Nation of Promise

Book two

Jack Barron

ISBN: 1-4826-6249-3
ISBN-13: 9781482662498

Table of Contents

Prologue

Aadil Achari, the President of India, sat in his office in New Delhi staring at the clock on the wall opposite him. His lips moved in silent prayer as the second hand swept inexorably toward the vertical. His heart thudded against his chest, and his palms were slick with sweat.

Achari was, as he had asked to be, completely alone, a state that had become unusual for him since he took office, and he tried to take comfort in the silence. He wondered if he would, or could, ever again feel comforted.

Precisely as the second hand reached twelve, Aadil Achari reached for the phone and pressed a button. He prayed for forgiveness as the call was answered, and he had to swallow twice before he could say, "Go."

As soon as he hung up, Achari bent forward until his elbows rested on his desk and used his hands to cover his ears. He could, he was sure, already hear the screams and the cries.

Tariq Khan, the President of Pakistan, and Raheem Malik, its Prime Minster, stood in one of the windows of the president's office, facing toward Mecca. They, too, were praying. The clock on the desk began to softly chime the hour, and a tear rolled down the prime minister's cheek. "Must we really," he asked, "do nothing?"

"We shall mourn," Tariq Khan replied. "That and nothing more."

John Barton sat by the stream that ran through The Preserve, the estate outside Atlanta, Georgia, his family had fostered and cherished for almost two hundred years. Dillon sat by his side. John's arm was around the dog's supple shoulders, and he stared at the water, saying nothing as he imagined the carnage taking place on the other side of the world.

Ultimately, the death and destruction must be laid at his door, for he had advised it, and his counsel had been followed. He remained certain that millions would be saved, yet, for their sakes, thousands were dead and dying.

John Barton fervently prayed for them, and for the strength to live with what he had wrought.

chapter

ONE

The tips of ancient branches, blanched white and stripped of their bark, still thrust bravely through the thick green cloak that strove to completely engulf them. The giant White Oak was dead, strangled by the kudzu vine that clung to it as closely as a lover. There was no doubt about it, although John Barton's heart broke just a little as the realization sank in. It was also another reminder of how long it had been since he and the red and black Shepherd known as Dillon Barton, were able to take a good long walk. John was shocked to realize just how much he had missed spending time overseeing The Preserve. Generations of his family had loved and cared for the beautiful plantation outside Atlanta, and John was proud to continue the tradition.

Dillon dashed out of the woods that bordered the winding path, his tail wagging wildly as he spotted his master. The dog flopped onto his haunches and leaned against John's leg, following his gaze.

"You see it too, don't you, boy? We were too late to save the tree, and I don't think anything can save the United States. We've lost both battles, and it's hard to take. That tree was alive when the Civil War was waged, and it died because of a weed. Kudzu. You can't let it get control. It strangled that tree as surely as liberal policies are strangling what was once a great nation, and the people aren't paying any more attention than the owner of that land."

John walked to the edge of the stream that divided The Preserve from the estate owned by Alan Donahue, the publisher of the left wing Atlanta Times. "Look," he said, and Dillon obediently trotted over and stood beside him. "Its roots reach the stream. One curve in the waterway, that tree would have been on the other bank, and on my land, I would have cared for it properly, and it would still be tall and strong."

The man heaved a deep sigh and, a mere second or two later, the dog did the same. John Barton reached down and stroked his long and pointed ears. "Sometimes, Dillon," he said, "I think you make more sense than most of the people in government, state or federal. Sometimes I feel like just coming home and spending the rest of my days here, with you and Catherine. It's not going to happen, no matter how much I think about it when I'm tired, or when I've had enough of being pilloried in the press. We have to put the battles behind us, Dillon, and get on with the war. We have to make sure that Georgia stays on the right side of the stream, or the whole darned state will meet the same fate as that oak. We got a fight on our hands, boy, and we have to see it through."

The dog barked once, as if in agreement, and the two security guards who now constantly shadowed the man expected to be the first president of the new Free State of Georgia, smiled.

"Wonder how the press would feel about this," one of them murmured to the other. "Think Georgia's ready for a president who chats with his dog?"

"Yup," the second guard replied. "Ah do. He's the only hope we've got, and Ah'm behind him all the way. The press won' be hearing about this from me. You?"

"No, siree," the first man said. "Mah wife would kill me."

Though he could not hear what they were saying, the sound of their voices reached former Georgia governor and former candidate for the Presidency of the USA, John Barton, and he turned and gave them a wave before he continued on the path that would circle The Preserve and take him back to the house.

"Don't think you're gonna be seeing much of me for a while, Dillon," he said to the dog, who was racing ahead of him, way out of earshot. "Sure hope you understand why."

A few hours later, John Barton sat in a padded chair, gazing at his reflection in the mirror in front of him. A white cloth was tucked into his shirt collar, and a TV makeup artist was busy dabbing foundation onto his skin. The cold damp sponge she was using felt far from pleasant.

"This won't take long, Governor," the young woman said, smiling at him in the mirror. "You don't need much. You already have a nice tan, and those blue eyes are gonna look right through the cameras and into people's hearts."

"Hope so, Christine," John said, glad he had glanced at her name tag before he sat down.

"I know so," the pretty blonde replied, applying a fine coat of spray to John's thick and waving head of hair.

"It get's grayer every day," John grumbled.

"And you'll get no sympathy from me," Christine said, laughing. "That's not gray, it's pure silver. It's gonna sparkle under the lights and, before this show is over, a few thousand more women out there will have fallen in love with you. There, you're done."

"Where do I go now?" John asked.

"Back to the green room," Christine told him, handing him his suit jacket. "They'll come and get you when they're ready for you. You remember the way?"

John nodded and thanked her before he left. The corridor down which he walked was floor to ceiling glass on one side, and downtown Atlanta, a mass of twinkling lights and tall buildings, was spread beneath him. From the street, the vast curving structure in which he stood would have dominated the skyline, arrogantly confirming WWN's supremacy when it came to keeping America and the rest of the globe informed about current events. Supremacy? Perhaps. World Wide News had certainly managed to establish that. The problem, when you looked at it from John's point of view, was the accuracy of the information, or rather the slant it was given before it was broadcast into billions of homes.

This was enemy territory. Mike Maunder, the impossibly wealthy owner of the Maunder Network, WWN's parent company, stood at one end of the political spectrum, and John Barton was firmly ensconced on the other. Maunder's employees thought like their boss. They had to, or they found themselves without their high paying jobs, and John did not expect any sympathy from Lenny Bling, the almost cadaverous late night talk show host whose guest he was scheduled to be. He also suspected that a good number of the calls to which he was to respond had been scheduled far in advance, with the person on the other end of the phone fully instructed on how to proceed.

John opened the door of the green room. Catherine, his beloved wife, sat in a sleekly contemporary armchair, a glass of juice on the coffee table in front of her, and a bank of monitors all but surrounding her.

"Guess I'm gonna get to watch you from angles even I've never seen before," she said as he crossed to her and sat down beside her.

"They'd do better to train those cameras on you," John commented, admiring the classical features that had grown even lovelier with age, the deep red hair swept back into a neat chignon, the pearls that decorate her ears and her neck, and the simple deep green sheath dress that flattered her trim and elegant figure and accentuated her emerald eyes. "Hard to find anyone who looks more like a First Lady."

"Why, thank you, honey," she said, reaching out to touch his hand. "You'd look quite presidential yourself if it wasn't for that diaper tucked under your chin."

The Bartons were still laughing when an earnest and excited young man, who looked as if he might have graduated from college the previous afternoon, arrived to escort John to the studio.

Christine was waiting on the set, ready to remove the cloth from his collar and dab a final layer of powder on his face. John was seated, and a tiny microphone was clipped to his clothing. He was asked to say a few words for the sound man, and then left to await the arrival of Mr. Bling. Seconds before airtime, the tall and skinny man strode onto the set and took his seat, dressed, as always, in shirt sleeves. He glared at John over his dark rimmed glasses, exhibiting all the warmth of a geriatric turtle peering myopically from its shell, and he said nothing. Nor did he smile until the floor manager pointed a finger at him and the light above one of the cameras went on.

Then, as if by magic, Lenny Bling suddenly exuded charm and sincerity. "My first guest tonight," he said, "is a most unusual man or, at least, a most unusual politician. Former Georgia governor, John Barton, recently and inexplicably dropped out of a possibly successful run for the White House. Having taken this drastic last minute step, for which the majority of the experts blame his party's loss in the subsequent election, he is now trying to persuade the citizens of his home state to ratify a plebiscite. It would authorize Georgia's secession from the Union, and allow it become an independent country. Some might call this treason."

Bling paused to once more glare contemptuously at John Barton, thereby making his own opinion more than evident. If he had hoped for a reaction from the former governor, he was sorely disappointed, so he was forced to continue, "Now, I am sure that many of you, like me, have kept abreast of this unique venture via the media. There are those few, we all know, who consider John Barton practically a candidate for sainthood, while others feel that he needs a good psychiatrist. Is John Barton a shameful turncoat, or is he merely deluded and more to be pitied than despised? Tonight, you will have the opportunity to make your own, sane decision."

'Oh, bravo!' John thought. *'So any person in his is her right mind should be convinced, by the end of this, that I'm either a traitor or a mental case. That's some choice. First blood to you, Bling.'*

"Edwina, get over here. You're missing it."

Edwina Boulder, the widow of a president, and herself now the President Elect of the United States of America, replaced the bottle of Pouilly Fuisse in the temperature controlled wine cellar tucked under the bar of her capacious New York City apartment, took her glass, strolled over to the off-white seating clustered around the huge wall mounted TV and settled herself on a chaise, plumping the pillows behind her before she nestled her head back against them.

"Should be fun," David Canton, Edwina's attorney, commented. "Bling's gonna take him to pieces."

"I wouldn't be too sure about that," Edwina said.

"Barton's a wily old bird," added Billy Hutzman, the veteran senator from New Jersey, who was known to Republicans as Billy Putzman. He was slated to become Minority Leader once the new regime was sworn in, and he had displaced Canton by becoming Edwina's closest confidante in the weeks since the election.

"Old, Billy?" Edwina asked. "The man's in his fifties. So am I, and so were you the last time I checked."

"Hush," Canton said. "I wanna hear what he has to say."

He was so engrossed in the screen in front of him that he failed to see the look Edwina Boulder shot him, though he wondered why a sudden chill crept up his spine.

"Governor Barton has agreed to speak with you, the viewers," Lenny Bling told the camera lens in front of him. "If you have questions or comments, please call the number on your screen."

He then turned towards John, and another camera broadcast a shot of the two of them, Bling intense and obviously disgusted by his guest, and John relaxed and at ease, waiting patiently for the inquisition to begin. "Let me recap, for a moment, Governor." Bling said. "This whole situation is so ... " He paused for a moment, theatrically and uncharacteristically searching for a word. "Well, the only term that comes to mind is bizarre, that I feel it merits repetition."

John nodded permission, and Bling went on, "You are pushing for a referendum, asking the citizens of Georgia to ratify leaving the federation we know as the United States of America and becoming an independent nation. Forgive me but, like most Americans, I thought this had all been settled in 1865, but no, here we go again. What are you doing, John, and, most importantly, why are you doing it."

"As to what I'm doing, Lenny," John said, smiling at his host, "I think you've just made that abundantly and succinctly clear. I doubt that anyone needs to hear it a third time. Why? That's a lot more complex. I'm not alone in this endeavor. Millions of Georgians feel that they are being badly served by the Federal Government in Washington, DC. Heck, it's not just Georgians. The recent campaign took me all across this land, and many of the people I met, from Maine to New Mexico, felt the same. The government, through many administrations, has failed to provide affordable energy. American homeowners have seen a sharp decline in the value of their property, the largest single investment most of them will ever make. They know that this is due to gross mismanagement on the part of Fannie Mae and Freddie Mac. Both were government agencies, and both are now bankrupt. And that's just the beginning. Everywhere we turn federal regulations are eroding more and more of our freedoms. Public employees have become the new upper income earners, while the rest of us are scrabbling for fewer and fewer private sector jobs."

"But ... " Bling broke in, but John refused to let him take control. "Let me finish answering the question, Lenny," he said. "Then we'll all know exactly where we stand, and we can go on from there."

Without resorting to outright hostility, Bling had no choice but to wave one hand, indicating that John should continue.

"The social security system is underfunded," he said, "and millions of Americans could well be facing an impoverished old age. The Medicare system is bankrupt. The welfare system functions so poorly that it is likely to grind to a halt, and that includes Section 8 housing, WIC, and food stamps. Billions of dollars are wasted annually in government grants for needless project, and the legal system is dysfunctional. If the United States of America were a corporation, it would have collapsed long ago, and the IRS and the Securities and Exchange Commission would be all over the CEO and his cronies, wondering who to first charge with malfeasance. That's just the tip of the iceberg, but it's a whole lot of good reasons for a fresh start."

"And that's it?" Bling asked, feigning amazement and doing a good job.

"That's it for now."

"Well then, Mr. Barton," Bling said, firmly emphasizing the 'mister', as if John no longer deserved to be called 'governor', "we thank you for that unique and very critical view of this great country, and we have a caller on the line. Marie in Oklahoma City, please go ahead."

"Governor," a female voice began, sounding as if it were reading from a script, "I'm the mother of three young children. Without Sooner care, the Medicaid program that pays their doctors; without the pay check my mother receives for her foster kids; my welfare check; our Section 8 housing voucher; my kids' free school lunch programs; LIHEAP energy assistance; and help from my church; my babies would be homeless, cold, and on the brink of starvation. I've heard that you want to take all this away, Governor. Sure you can do it, but only if you're willing to have my dead kids on your conscience. Maybe you are, but what kind of a man does that make you?"

John refused to rise to the bait. "May I ask," he calmly inquired, "why you have not mentioned your children's father? Is he not part of their lives?"

"I dunno who their dads are," Marie yelled, speaking for herself now, "and it don't matter. You got no right to ask that question. I'm in charge, and I'm responsible for my kids."

"With all due respect, ma'am," John said, "it doesn't sound that way to me. It sounds as if you've made your fellow citizens, the ones who work and pay taxes, responsible for your family. With the people's approval, the Free State of Georgia will have a new constitution. Under its provisions, your family's needs will be met by the private charity partnerships we will develop, and the 'people to people' network we shall establish. Welfare recipients will find new purpose in their lives as they help themselves and others to live without assistance."

"Oh, yeah," Marie broke in, "and how you gonna do that? I got no education. How'm I gonna get a job?"

"You will be taught the skills you need, according to your abilities and your interests. In the beginning, you will assist others who are being educated, and you will continue to receive government assistance while you do so. You will provide child care and meal preparation, and you will perform household duties. Others, in their turn, will do the same for you. Eventually, you will find a job, and the responsibility for your family will then move from the hands of your fellow citizens into your own. At that point, you truly will be in charge."

"And until then I can go back to being a slave?" Marie asked. "No thanks, Governor. Think I'll stay right where

I am. And you want to call this a 'free state'? I aint so sure about that."

"Thanks for the input, Marie." John said.

"Let's hope," Bling said, "that the citizens of Georgia are with us tonight, and that they are appreciating the details of the Brave New World John Barton wants them to inhabit. Sonny from New York, you're on the air."

"Hey, Govnuh," a man who unmistakably hailed from deepest Brooklyn yelled into the phone, "I'm a lawyer here in duh Big Apple. Been reading about the legal parts of your plan for Georgia. Wha'dis 'loser pays' thing? You mean that if I sue someone, for a client of mine, and dey beat us in court, dey can come after my client for the money they laid out for their defense? Hell, far as I can tell, in some cases dey can even come after me! You've lost it, Govnuh, if you ever had it to start with. How d'ya think the poor are gonna get any justice around here, and what about duh lawyers? You wan' us to pay?"

"If you bring frivolous suits, maybe you should," John said. "Look, Sonny, it would take far longer than Lenny has for me to fully answer you. Let me just say that England has a

Loser Pay system, and it seems to work for them."

"Yeah," Sonny said, "and dey got a lotta broke lawyers, too."

"Well," John said, "I don't know about broke, but they may well be more cautious, and I don't think that's a bad thing. Our courts are glutted with damage suits brought by people who slipped on ice or wet floors, spilled hot coffee, or don't like where the plastic surgeon left their navel. Most of them belong more with the insurance companies than they do with the courts. Our new constitution will replace many current public systems with new insurance programs. They will provide coverage, but they will also oversee inspections and mandate that their customers improve their safety standards if they wish to remain insured. Non-insured businesses and professionals, such as lawyers and doctors, will pay into a liability pool that will protect the individuals and other businesses they may harm. So, those with claims will be able to go straight to the insurer, clearing our court dockets, receiving better settlements and saving the thirty-three percent attorneys customarily charge. It will be in the insurers' best interest to have their clients run the most risk free operations they can, and the state will assist by giving tax cuts to those businesses with the fewest claims against them."

"Lotsa luck, Barton," Sonny growled. "Glad I aint movin' to Atlanta. I'd be waiting tables jus'ta pay my student loans. Tell your lawyers that a coupl'a d'em can room with me while dey're looking for work up here."

"I'll pass on that message, Sonny," John said, laughing.

"Glad you're amused, John," Bling said. "Most of us would regard ripping apart society's fabric and replacing it with a new and shoddy cloth as a far more serious undertaking."

He turned sharply away, and informed his camera that he would return after a short break.

The makeup staff leapt upon them, powdering and primping, and it seemed only seconds before Bling welcomed his audience back and informed John that Jane in Texas was ready to speak with him.

The woman sounded calm and genuinely interested, and she spoke softly when she said, "I'm a tenth grade teacher. If I were to move to the new nation you propose, would I see differences between your educational system and the one in place here in Houston?"

"Yes, Jane, you would." John Barton said. "All our schools will be private. Students between the ages of six and eighteen will each receive a voucher for every school year. They and their parents will then be able to select from a variety of schools. In order to accept the vouchers, schools will have to meet the accreditation standards established by a board of regents similar to the ones governing hospitals. The government's only jobs will be supplying the vouchers, establishing the standards and overseeing the teachers' professional licensing program. Although any school will be able to choose being totally private, those who do not do so must have at least half their students participating under the voucher system."

"So no more nit picking school boards or Napoleonic superintendants?" Jane asked.

John laughed again. "Great description, Jane, and you're right. You would be treated like all other employees in the private sector and, like them, receive a salary commensurate to your skills. It would be far easier for you to find another school, if the one you were in did not prove congenial. All schools would be private businesses and operate as such."

"I have to tell you, Governor, that it makes sense to me," Jane said. "I spend more than half my time coaching students so they can take ill conceived state mandated tests. They really prove nothing about the kids' educational level, but our funding depends on the results. It would be nice to be able to actually teach again. I even have trouble testing my kids. I can't ask them to study on any night when one of the athletic teams is practicing. They have to be able to devote all their energies to the sport. There are practices Monday through Thursday. When are these kids going to get an education? They can't all go to college on football scholarships."

"You know, I hadn't thought of that, and I agree with you," John Barton said, leaning forward and directly addressing the woman he could almost see on the other end of the camera lens. "Why shouldn't we separate academics and athletics, at least on a pre-college level? Why can't businesses and corporations sponsor these teams, providing coaching, equipment and transportation, and using the existing school athletic facilities on the weekends and during the breaks? We could then use the school's physical education time to keep the team members and the other kids in shape, and cut down on some enormous expenses. It appalls me to read that a school's library purchases have been cut, so that the basketball team can have new uniforms. Thank you, Jane. You've just contributed to the formation of a new land."

"Thank you, Governor," Jane said. "I'm flattered and pleased to have helped, and your new Georgia sounds pretty attractive to me."

An obviously annoyed Lenny Bling called for an immediate and unscheduled commercial break. In less than a minute, representatives from nine giant corporations called in, expressing interest in being part of the program and asking that Governor Barton contact them. The floor manager whispered the news into Bling's ear just before the show resumed. It did nothing to improve his mood.

"I'm beginning to feel as if I've fallen down a rabbit hole," he told his audience, "and I haven't ended up in Wonderland. Let's see if a doctor in Canada can restore some sanity to these proceedings. Hello, sir, you're on the air with Governor Barton."

"Hello, John Barton," the man said. "I'm sure you know that we have a national health system here in Canada, and it takes care of everyone. Now, the US courts have decided that the health care plan the congress passed is unconstitutional. That leaves America currently in the private sector and with millions still uninsured. What will your new nation do for its citizens' health care needs?"

"Your system takes care of everyone?" John asked. "Well, I suppose you could say that if you don't mind waiting six months for an MRI, or up to two years for many elective surgeries. I, personally, would not want to be part of your plan, nor would I want my family included."

"Okay," the Canadian said, "but the sick and the injured have to be treated. What do you propose?"

"In all honesty," John said, "we're still working on this one. I have established a fact finding committee, chaired by Peter Haven, the president of one of Atlanta's major health care complexes. The current blueprint, which has not been finalized, proposes the establishment of many private medical clinics, and a government subsidized payment plan for the poor and indigent. Each citizen will have an identification card. It will be necessary to produce it in order to vote, and it will also entitle the bearer to seek care at any facility they choose. However, should you go to an emergency room for something as simple as a cold, or a minor injury, you will be directed to the nearest clinic for treatment."

"Sounds okay on the surface," Bling chimed in, "but who's going to want to invest in clinics in the inner city areas?"

"I don't think we'll have a problem with that," John said, "even if it means initially subsidizing existing charity clinics. And yes, before either of you says anything, I am aware that this means that some people will be seeing doctors who have better training and skills than others. It is my firm belief, and it is in keeping with our new constitution, that we must, above all, in order for this new nation to grow, encourage greatness for each individual and merit based pay. The surgeon who continuously seeks training in new advances, who works with the latest equipment, utilizing the most up to date drugs and medical devices, deserves to charge more than a colleague who remains static. We know that all innovations are, at first, costly, but we confidently expect that, once they are in greater supply, they will filter down and become available to the masses at a price they can afford. It happens with goods all the time, so why not with medical services? It definitely did when it comes to Lasik surgery."

"I'm wondering, John," Bling said, "if the good doctor shares your confidence. I'm not sure that I do."

He quickly ended the segment, smirking as he said, "Will there be a Free State of Georgia? No one knows, though the doubters appear to outnumber those who believe there will. Let us bid Governor John Barton goodnight, and invite him to return after the plebiscite is completed. I, for one, shall be interested in his reaction once the people of this American state have spoken."

'And you confidently expect,' John thought, *'to be able to serve me a large plate of crow, and watch me eat it. Better bring a fork for yourself, just in case you need it.'*

chapter

TWO

"Still don't see why you declined the second segment," David Canton said.

Edwina Boulder sat up, reached for the remote, and turned off the TV. "No," she said, "I am sure that you don't. Billy, how about you?"

"Whole lot of good reason, baby," Billy Hutzman said, smiling. Edwina winced at the endearment, and he quickly decided not to be so familiar in the future. Edwina Boulder did not appreciate anything that called attention to her femininity which, Billy thought, was hardly surprising when one considered how little of it there was. No wonder her husband had screwed his way through a gubernatorial mansion *and* the house at 1600 Pennsylvania Avenue. Still,

Billy had to admit, the interns had been far better looking in those days.

He glanced over at Edwina, who was tapping her nails on a vast expanse of glass coffee table, impatiently waiting for his answer. Pale brown hair cut in a businesslike bob and tucked behind her ears, her glance fiercely intelligent and colder than an Arctic ice floe, she wore another of her perennial pants suits, all, it seemed, either gray, black or tan, and all cut so that they did nothing to flatter her ever widening hips. Billy wondered, not for the first time, what the voters saw in her. And she was as unpleasant as she was unattractive. Still, she was going to be president, and that new Chief of Staff of hers, now she was worth hanging about for.

"What are you smiling at, Billy?"

"Me?" Billy Hutzman tore himself from a reverie that involved impossibly long coffee colored legs wrapped around him like ivy and struggled to remember what he and the President Elect had been discussing. "Me? Nothing, except that you're going to get exactly what you want just one more time."

"I usually do," Edwina agreed. "Always have. Would you care to explain to my esteemed legal expert exactly what that entails?"

Billy got up and strolled over to one of the long windows. The apartments on this side of The Dakota had a wonderful view of New York's Central Park. Billy loved the old building, with its ornate woodwork, crown moldings, carved fireplaces and coffered ceilings, and he hated the way Edwina's starkly contemporary furniture clashed with its timeless elegance. But then, Edwina thoroughly enjoyed clashing.

"You did not appear on Bling's second segment," he said, staring at his reflection in the glass, with millions of lights twinkling through him as if he were some phantasm come to lord it over the city from on high, "because to follow Barton would look defensive. You will be president, and he is a loser, if only by default. You are also currently fostering a sense of mystique. Playing a low profile. Keeping the press and public waiting until, by Inaugural Day, they are thirsting for a sight of you. You are using the time to plan strategy, and you are doing it well. You needed a rest after the campaign, and you have all those briefings to attend before you take office. That's enough for now."

Billy turned his back on the window, though he stayed where he was, his slight body surrounded by lights that silvered the normally dull gray in his hair, and his expression concealed by the glow behind him. His ears were pronounced and slightly pointed, which gave him, in silhouette, an elfin air, or, perhaps, a touch of Mephistopheles.

"Those are the obvious reasons," he continued. "The ones you would share with anyone close to you who asked. They have, however, absolutely nothing to do with the truth."

David Canton said, "I don't get it." Edwina brayed, which, for her, passed for laughter, and clapped her hands.

"I knew you'd see it, Billy," she said. "Just as well as I knew he wouldn't. You want to tell him?"

"Up to you," Billy said. "You're in charge."

"Yes, I am, aren't I?" Edwina said. "And, by God, it feels good. You tell him. I hate explaining."

"She wants Barton to succeed."

"In seceding?" Canton asked.

"We are not playing word games, David," Edwina snapped. "Shut up and listen. Go ahead, Billy. He won't interrupt again."

David Canton tried to slump further back into his chair. Unfortunately, he was about a hundred and fifty pounds short of any chance of success.

"The President Elect," Billy continued, taking a seat at the desk that was centered in front of the bayed out windows and noticing, for the first time, how reminiscent of the Oval Office the arrangement was, "is willing, no eager, for John Barton to have his way. She calculates, and probably correctly, that a number of the Bible Belt states will follow Georgia's example over the next year or so, each of them becoming either a separate nation or a member of a new confederacy, and I do not use the word lightly."

Canton glanced at Edwina and, without looking at him, she lowered her chin by a smidgen of inch, granting him permission to speak.

"And this is good thing?" Canton asked, frowning in puzzlement until his porcine eyes all but disappeared among folds of skin.

"If you're Edwina, it is." Hutzman said, toying with a silk lined presentation box that preserved, under glass, the pen Edwina's husband had used to sign some piece of legislation. It had probably seemed monumental at the time, but it was, by now, almost entirely forgotten. "Those states are hot beds of far right wing politics. They are one vast Tea Party, and they make the most died in the wool northern Republicans look liberal by comparison. Get rid of 'em, and she'll have her own way with precious little opposition."

"But that's dissolving the union," Canton spluttered.

"No, David," Edwina said, "I prefer to think of it as a division, not dissolution. Why should we continue to provide public services to rural communities filled with rednecks who contribute precious little to the economy? Let them take care of their own."

"But you are from the south," Canton protested.

"So who better to know it for what it is?" She responded. "Florida will stay with us. It's just New York with better weather, anyway. And the rest of them? Texas is a land of its own. Always has been and, aside from NASA and the Houston medical centers, it's twenty years behind a lot of third world countries. Let them live in the land time forgot, thinking like characters in The Scarlet Letter while they're behaving like leftovers from Tobacco Road, and who needs Georgia, Mississippi, Louisiana, Alabama or Arkansas? Most of the industry they have is only there because it moved from the north when it was offered huge tax breaks. Take supporting the south out of the equation, and there'll be plenty in the budget to lure all those businesses back up here. Hell, most of what went there was polluting the atmosphere on a twenty-four seven basis. Might be better if it stayed where it is and choked a cracker or two, instead of choking us."

Canton could think of nothing to say, so Billy broke the silence. "And that, my friend, is the cake and the frosting. If we end up losing a few more conservative states, the shift in power in Washington will make it all the more easy for Edwina to make the kind of deals she wants, with whomever she wants, without those right wing watchdogs nitpicking us on every new program or deal we come up with. And on top of all this,

Madame President has saved the cherry for last."

"Ah, Billy boy," Edwina said, finishing her wine and crossing to the bar, "I'm beginning to think that you read my mind. Question is, are you one step behind me, or one step ahead?"

"Take a better politician than me to get ahead of you, Edwina," Billy said, silently reminding himself to push a little harder on the dumb button from then on. "You take the coup de grace. You're the one who figured it out."

Edwina removed a frosted Lalique glass from the bar's freezer draw, filled it with wine and raised it to the light, admiring the golden glow of the vintage. "They will not be able to support themselves," she said, "so they will be forced to seek loans. They'll have nowhere else to go, I will see to that, so they will have to come to us. They will then need to keep paying us interest and, whenever we get the chance, we'll jack up the rate.It may bankrupt them. Sad, but these things happen."

The President Elect of the United States tipped her glass toward her audience, as if acknowledging a thunderous round of applause, smiled briefly and drank.

Carolyn McKay fell asleep kissing the emerald ring on the third finger of her left hand. Iacovus Eliades, who had placed it there a mere couple of hours earlier, lifted a long strand of setter red hair from her cheek and held it for a moment before he laid it carefully on the masses of soft curls that spilled over the pillow. She was so beautiful, and she looked, he thought, more like an innocent child than a woman worth billions who funded and headed what was fast becoming one of the world's largest charities.

Carolyn's father had never married again after his wife was killed in a car accident when their child was just a few months old, and his last words to Carolyn, many years later, had been an apology for her lack of a mother's love. Carolyn, who was in her thirties then, was still painfully shy, but she had overcome this to found 'A Mother's Love' in memory of both her parents. Wherever there were children in need, be they starving, maimed or desperately ill, there was Carolyn, dispensing endless affection, energy, time and money in about equal amounts.

Jim Eliades sometimes thought he would drown in his admiration for her before he drowned in his love, and he wasn't quite sure which fate he would prefer.

Jim, who came from a fiercely Greek family, most of whom still lived in New York's Hudson Valley, had been John Barton's gubernatorial chief of staff, and he was now his campaign manager, which meant he had precious little free time. His laptop case was leaning against the bedside table, but he ignored it for a moment, stretched out beside Carolyn, took her hand and thanked God that she was there.

They'd met because of the presidential campaign. Jim was seldom far from John Barton's side, and Carolyn was one of a devoted core of supporters and a member of the board of St. Mark's church. John was its chairman.

Jim had barely noticed her at first. He'd been obsessed with work and with a woman he'd thought was the love of his life. A woman who had proved to be a liar, a spy dedicated to John's destruction, and a lesbian.

Jim's self-respect had hit a new low, and he'd seen the world from the wrong side of a bottle for a while. Then, late one night, he'd sat down to talk to Carolyn, on the jet that proved to be her own, and it was as if the jagged edges of his life were suddenly smooth and he was at peace with the world.

They had spent most of their free time together ever since, slowly getting to know one another, learning to trust, learning to love. It was during her third trip overseas that he realized how much he missed her, and how incomplete he was when she was gone from his side. It was then that he made his decision.

God, how he loved her. He had planned his proposal for the last couple of months; waiting for a friend who made regular business trips to Brazil to track down a perfect stone as deeply glowing as her eyes; waiting for the jewelers to set it exactly as he wanted, between diamonds taken from her mother's engagement ring; waiting for Carolyn to come home from Rawanda.

Her plane had landed at just after four, and he was there to greet her. He drove her to the Atlanta Botanical Garden and held her close as they walked paths that, even in January, were lined with blossoms. They said little, and he knew she was too exhausted to even ask why they were there. She gave so much of herself on these trips.

The sun had set by the time they neared the Robinson Gazebo, and the path was suddenly and magically lighted for them. At its end, the glass roof glowed above them, lit by the stars and rising moon, and Atlanta's skyline shimmered on one side, mirrored in the aquatic plant pool on the other. Soft music played and, at the gazebo's center, a table was set for two, white damask cloth cascading to the floor and a gardenia centerpiece, dotted with tiny candles, scenting the air. Next to it, logs burned in a brazier, bright flames holding back the evening chill.

Carolyn gasped in surprise.

Jim seated her, and the chef from his favorite Greek restaurant presented an endless array of delicacies, ending with pastries so flaky that the crumbs were born away on the breeze and dense, rich coffee in tiny cups.

Carolyn sighed with contentment. "What a perfect evening. Is it my birthday, or yours? Or is it Christmas all over again?"

"None of the above," Jim said. "Each of those marks the end of a year, and I am hoping that this is a beginning."

"Of what?" she asked and, a moment later, he was on his knees at her feet. He could not quite remember what he said as he poured out his heart. It did not matter for, when he was done, she smiled down at him and nodded.

He took her home then, and he went inside with her, clasping her hand so tightly that he could feel the ring on her finger. Her staff greeted them, took one look at their faces and quietly disappeared. They found themselves in her bedroom, and what followed seemed only right and proper.

It was their first time together and, for her, it was the first meaningful time ever.

Jim Eliades was sure he was holding the entire globe cradled in the palm of his hand.

He leaned over and kissed Carolyn's cheek, set pillows against the headboard, took out his laptop, switched it on and prepared to work. John and Catherine were almost through with the national TV bit, and it was time to bring this campaign home.

Martine Rivers doubted that she could want for more. Chief of Staff to the President Elect. It couldn't get much better. Her office adjoined her bedroom in Edwina's apartment, and it would adjoin a far larger oval room in just a couple of weeks.

She'd made it. She hacked and clawed, and lied and cheated and manipulated, and it had all been worth it. She was young, affluent, educated, spectacularly beautiful, and about to move slap damn into the center of the public eye. She intended to remain there.

Martine Rivers had it all.

As she scrolled down her computer screen, checking Edwina's calendar for the next few days, her cell phone, which was lying next to her on the desk, began a vibrating dance across the polished marble surface. Martine picked it up, checked the screen and touched 'talk', sighing as she did so.

"Hello Daddy."

"Martine. Where are you?"

"New York City. Why is that the first question anyone ever asks me?"

"Because no one ever knows the answer, I presume," her father said. "And I take it that you will be going from there to DC?"

"Mmmm, hmmm, right before the inauguration."

"And you are sure that this is what you want?"

"Yes, Daddy, I am."

"Your mother and I are concerned."

"Still don't trust the Democrats?"

"There is no need to be sarcastic, Martine," her father said, obviously making an effort to control his famous temper, which was as short-lived as it was explosive. "We shall not be the first family to disagree politically. It is natural that we should see things differently. Your mother and I worked hard for our success, in a time when it was hard for people of our race to rise above the crowd."

"While I have taken money and privilege for granted," Martine countered. "I know, Daddy. I've heard it all before. You don't trust us to protect your assets, and you're sure John Barton will."

"As sure as I can be," Augustin Rivers said. "At least the chances are far better. And what does your employer feel about the possibility of us finding ourselves living in different countries?"

"Don't know, Daddy. And, if I did, I wouldn't tell you."

"No reason not to," her father said. "Barton doesn't have to call me for advice."

"No," Martine said, her voice softening, "he's got Jim Eliades to turn to for that."

"Who? Never mind. Well, I doubt that we shall see you soon, except on the television. Please know that your mother and I are here if you need us, and give our regards to Sandy. If you are still seeing her, that is."

Martine's father ended the call. She stared at her phone. It wasn't often they surprised her, though they'd accepted the news of her liberal leanings more stoically than she'd expected. This, on the other hand, was a bombshell.

She'd had no idea they knew she was a lesbian.

"And what the hell are you doin' in Chicago?" Dallas Dee Trelawney demanded. "Them northern city slickers aint voting in this referendum. You need to get your butt back to Georgia, and bring Catherine's with ya'."

"We'll be there tomorrow, Dallas Dee," John Barton said. "And we won't leave again until this is over."

"Guess that'll have to be good enough," Dallas Dee grudgingly conceded. "Damned if I can see what y'all are doing up there anyway."

"Come on, Dallas, we all discussed it, you know that. We need national recognition of what we're trying to do, and I think as many Georgians watch Bling and Mapo as people do anywhere else."

"Texans got more sense," Dallas Dee grumbled.

"Mizz Trelawney," John protested, glad that the salty and prickly multi-millionairess on the other end of the line could not see his grin, "I do believe that you misstate the case. You, ma'am, have become as much of Georgian as I am since you did us the honor of moving to our fair state, and that is saying something. And even you cannot speak for all Texans."

"Quit talkin' like a lawyer," Dallas Dee said. "Can't stand any of 'em, even my own. Coupl'a more minutes, and you'll be soundin' like a politician. God knows what'll happen to us all then."

"Let's not find out," John said. "I'll be at the St. Mark's board meeting on Thursday. We'll talk then. Gotta go. The show is starting."

"What? Didn't realize it was that time already."

"Why, Dallas Dee," John said, feigning amazement, "I do believe that you are planning to watch."

"Only 'cause of Catherine," Dallas growled. "Wouldn't waste the electricity otherwise."

The line went dead, and John turned to the monitor in front of him. He found being in the television studios rather interesting. One got to see the bits behind the production. The mechanics the viewers at home never witnessed. Right now, an announcer in a suit that looked as if it must have cost a small fortune, though it had obviously not been tailored for him, and the jacket collar stood too far away from his neck, was working the audience into the proper degree of frenzy to greet their host. His black hair gleamed under the lights as if it had been coated in petroleum jelly, and he had been carefully chosen to appeal to every possible segment of the audience. African, Hispanic and Caucasian blood obviously ran through his veins, and John would not have been surprised to find that his DNA had been tested for traces of American Indian and Asian genes. The man was undeniably good looking. This and his rich baritone made him the focus of all eyes, at least for the present.

"Ladies and gentlemen, my name is Antoine and, in just a few moments, it will be my pleasure and honor to ask you to rise to your feet, if that's what you feel like doing, and we hope it is, and welcome the first lady of American television. She's an author, a publisher, an entrepreneur, a producer, an actress, and the winner of too many awards to mention. She's a philanthropist and a guest, every day, in millions of homes worldwide."

The floor manager pointed a finger at him, beginning a count down on his fingers, and Antoine's voice rose to an almost impossibly excited pitch as he announced, "She's the friend of presidents, princes, prime ministers and popes. And she's a friend of yours. And here she is, ladies and gentleman. Other's may call her Ms. Wilson, but to you, she just your MAAAAAAYYYYY POOOOOOOOOOOH!"

None of this went out on the air, so it seemed as if the woman who walked out onto the set had inspired a tsunami of adoration simply by her appearance, and perhaps she would have done so anyway.

For millions, Mapo Wilson personified the American dream. Poor, black and sexually abused as a child, she had used her talent for communication, her almost uncanny ability to appear as if she were using the camera lens to connect with each viewer on a personal and individual basis, and risen to become the wealthiest self-made woman in the nation, and one of the richest in the world.

One could not help but admire her, even if one deplored her politics as much as John and Catherine Barton did. His wife, John thought, was about to walk into the lion's den, and she was doing it all on her own.

Mapo blew kisses and waved, bathing for a moment in the rush the applause must have given her. Then she waved her hands for silence and, as soon as she could possibly be heard over the roar of the crowd, said, "Oh, my God! Thank you! Thank you! I love you all!"

The woman bounced to her chair and sat down, crossing neat ankles. She was exquisitely dressed, hiding the fact that she fought a continual battle with overweight, and her hair and makeup were perfect. She had actually grown far better looking in the years since she had come to national prominence, and John was forced to wonder how much expert and subtle cosmetic surgery had been a part of this.

Mapo settled herself, and her audience seated themselves. "Now," she said once all was quiet, "the first thing I have to do is apologize. I promised, yesterday, that I would bring pictures of my lunch with the Dalai Lama and my dinner with Nelson Mandela. I wanted to show you how wonderfully these two incredible men have aged. They have written on their faces all the experience and wisdom they have accumulated over the years, and it is a privilege just to sit and gaze at them. I feel so lucky that I was able to set aside the time to meet with each of them. Y'all know how busy my days are, and I was in a rush this morning. Left those photographs in my dressing room at home. You know how it is, ladies, too many things on our minds all at once."

Mapo looked helpless and contrite, and the audience murmured its agreement and sympathy and applauded.

"So," Mapo went on. "No great men today, not even in pictures. Instead, my first guest is a woman and the wife of a failed presidential candidate. Talk about going from the sublime to the ridiculous, huh?"

The audience dutifully picked up on its cue and laughed, managing to sound nicely derisive. Mapo beamed her approval.

"Catherine Barton," she continued, addressing the lens as if it were her nearest and dearest, while somehow still managing to include the audience, "is a mother and a grand-mother. She is also the wife of John Barton."

Mapo paused and raised a delightfully quizzical and exquisitely winged eyebrow. "Do I see puzzled looks?" She asked. "Surely not?" Don't you follow extreme right wing politics as avidly as I do?"

There was a ripple of laughter, and a camera picked up shots of the audience members enthusiastically shaking their heads.

"John Barton. Some of you at least must remember."

There were nods, and Mapo smiled encouragingly and said, "That's it. The guy who had the b … .., um, guts to run against our fabulous President Elect, Edwina Boulder. Dropped out at the last minute. Guess he couldn't stomach getting his nose rubbed at those polls. We'll have to ask Mrs. Barton about that. Anyway, all those fanatics among you must know that the Bartons are spearheading the push for a plebiscite vote in the state of Georgia. If they get their way, that state will then secede from the Union, and John Barton will likely become its first president."

Boos and catcalls greeted this, and Mapo raised her hands in mock horror. "Please, please, don't do this. Don't we always try to be fair and open minded here? Well, we don't want to be any different today so, without further ado, let me introduce Catherine Barton, the wife of the man many are calling the Anti-American Candidate."

Catherine stepped into the light, to be greeted by a chorus of boos, hisses and whistles. She paused, letting the audience absorb the simple elegance of her Escada suit, the Tahitian pearls that encircled her neck, the hair twisted on her head until it resembled a crown, and her air of utter and sublime calm.

"Dear God,' John silently prayed, "isn't she incredible, this creation of Yours? How many women would have the courage to stand there like that and let them hate her? Stay with her, Lord. She needs You now."

Catherine walked to her chair and sat down. Mapo did not rise to greet her, and she gave the audience plenty of time to vent its scorn before she said, "Welcome, Catherine, or should I call you Mrs. Barton?"

"No, no," Catherine said, her smile rivaling the studio lights. "Please call me Catherine. Anything else would seem strange. I've been such a regular viewer that I feel as if I've known you for years. Almost as if we raised my children together."

Mapo looked her guest in the eye for the first time, reassessing her. This might just be a worthy opponent. Managing to draw attention to her age and the fact that, mere decades ago, taking care of someone else's house and kids might have been her only employment opportunity was masterful, particularly when it was accomplished the first time those perfect lips parted.

"Well, Catherine," she said, leaning back in her chair, "I'm pretty sure we've never met." She didn't add, 'Thank God', but her face said it for her, and there were a few titters. "We probably don't attend the same political functions." She held up a pile of papers. "These are questions submitted by this audience and the visitors to my web site. They're still pouring in there, so let's get right down to it." She waved the pages and selected one, as if at random. "Ah, here's a concern many of us must share. In the event that a new constitution is enacted in Georgia, how will abortion and gay rights be handled under the new laws?"

"Oh, my, Mapo," Catherine said, "how like you not to waste any time before getting to two of the most contentious issues of our time. Like you, I won't beat around the bush. John and I are what you would term pro-life, as are many of our supporters. However, we want to found a nation that allows its citizens more freedom to assume personal responsibility than any other on the face of this earth. One of the most important aspects of this is self-determination when it comes to medical decisions. The state will not interfere in these matters, unless a pregnancy is far enough advanced that the infant concerned is viable, and capable of existing on its own outside the womb, either with or without medical intervention. Once the baby reaches that threshold, it will be deemed a living human being, and normal infanticide statutes will come into force. As for gay rights, all citizens of this new land will be regarded as equal. No one will be deprived of rights, nor will there be any special privileges or programs for any one segment of the population. We shall truly be one people under God."

Catherine stopped speaking, and there was silence for a second. Then the audience began round after round of wild applause. Mapo looked shocked for an instant, and then quickly called for a commercial break. Wholehearted approval was not what she had wanted, or expected, to display to millions.

It was Mapo who was fidgeting with papers when the broadcast resumed. Catherine's hands were loosely clasped in her lap, and she was waiting good-naturedly for the proceedings to resume.

"Thank you for so honestly answering the abortion segment of my question, Catherine. Now, how will you handle gay marriage?"

"We won't," Catherine said, shrugging lightly.

"I beg your pardon?" Mapo said, drawing herself up and looking shocked. "Am I to understand that there will be no gay marriage in this new country, or perhaps there just won't be any gay people ... or any whose skins aren't white?"

Catherine laughed out loud. "Why I just love your wit, Mapo. Always have. Imagine deporting that many people. Why, who'd think of such a thing? It's just as I said," she was suddenly serious, "one nation, one people, each of them equal under God and their government. We're butting out of private business, and that includes marriage."

"The state will have nothing to do with marriage?" Mapo asked, aghast. "But government has been involved in licensing and mandating the acceptable forms of marriage since this nation began. How can you do that?"

"But *this* is a new nation," Catherine rejoined, "with new ways. No one will be prohibited, once they reach majority, from freely entering into any legal and binding contract. That, after all, is what marriage actually is. No matter what your faith, or which religious ceremony is performed when you wed, you are not married until you sign the contract known as the marriage certificate. Should you wish to break that bond, you must go to the courts, not the ministers. Am I right?"

Now it was Catherine who turned to the audience and invited a response. There were nods, and a number of people voiced their agreement.

"The French, for instance," Catherine continued, "can celebrate their marriage in any church they please, or none. That ceremony does not construe a legal marriage. That contract can only be entered into at the office of the mayor. You and I, Mapo, and others of our age, will remember Grace Kelly and Prince Rainier walking to that office, so that they could be legally wed."

Mapo would have liked to deny any such recollection, but someone would have been bound to do the research and call her on it, so she said nothing.

"Similarly," Catherine went on, "any two citizens of the Free State of Georgia will be able to come to an agreement, much like the one we now call a pre-nuptial, and it will be drawn up by an attorney, duly signed, notarized, and properly registered with the Secretary of State."

Mapo leapt on this as avidly as a starving bloodhound might seize a porterhouse. "And what about those who can't afford an attorney," she sneered. "Will they be deprived of the privilege of this soulless travesty of a marriage?"

"Oh, no," Catherine said in the tone she might have applied to a three year old who asked if the Bogey Man really lived under the bed. "Of course not. The necessary documents will be available on line, or at book stores. A couple will be able to fill them out, take them to a government office and pay a small filing fee. The result will be just the same, and many without large incomes to protect will probably choose this alternative."

"And where does that leave those of us who believe that our union should be blessed by God," Mapo asked.

"We share your belief," Catherine said, "and we hope that all our citizens will do the same, though we shall not force them. Nothing in the constitution will preclude the celebration of a marriage in a church or other place of worship, or in your backyard, or on the shores of the ocean or one or our beautiful lakes. As with many of our new provisions, the average citizen will probably not even notice the difference."

The audience was quiet now, concentrating on her words and subconsciously nodding agreement with them.

Mapo took one more shot. "Okay," she said, 'but what about social security benefits, pensions, or insurances that normally go to a surviving spouse, most often the wife? Both in the event that the marriage continues, and if there is a divorce."

"Nothing," Catherine said, shrugging again. "No lawyers involved to argue about it, if that's what you mean. It will all have been covered in the marriage contract, and that is how it will be." She turned to the audience once more. "Won't it be nice to have life made so simple?"

They applauded, and they cried out their approval. John watched, beaming. It seemed as if Catherine was in charge of the show, and Mapo was merely an assistant, taking care of the nuts and bolts of television.

"We have a question from Margaret, from Ohio," the lady in question interjected, fighting to regain control. "How will you tackle the high price of energy?"

Catherine thought for a moment before she said, "I don't want to give you a simplistic answer or make it seem as if this problem will be solved overnight, but there is a lot we can do to bring down energy prices. Way back when I was in college, some time just after the Flood ... " She was interrupted by giggles from the crowd, and she acknowledged them with another of those high voltage smiles. "I took Econ 101. One of the lectures I attended has remained true over all these years. The rules of supply and demand still stand firm. If supply increases and demand decreases, the prices drop. So, based on that theory, we need to increase supply and reduce demand."

"And just how will you and your husband manage that?" Mapo asked her tone sodden with sarcasm.

"I shan't," Catherine responded, "but the new Georgia's elected officials will. For almost half a century we have been equipping the U.S. Navy's submarine fleet with small nuclear powered systems that operate safely and efficiently. We can take that same type of system, which is now manufactured by several internationally reliable companies, and install units throughout Georgia, in small towns, big cities and wherever we can put them. The use of these small generators will make a big difference in our electricity costs and the available supply. We will not have a large and inefficient, bureaucratic Nuclear Regulatory Commission breathing down our necks, so we will be able to proceed safely and rapidly. John and the new energy commission will also be pushing for automobiles, buses and trucks to run on natural gas and electricity and, of course, the use of solar and wind power where applicable."

The audience took a collective pause, trying to see the downside to this. It failed, so it applauded, rather remarkably warmly.

Mapo stood up, bringing the acclamation to an abrupt halt, and said, "I'm not so sure that you will manage to remain so cozily in background, Mrs. Barton. But let's move on. Joe from Missouri wants to know if the nation of Georgia will continue United States foreign policy."

"I'm no diplomat," Catherine said, and an audience member shouted, "Oh, yes, you are!"

There was laughter, and more applause before Catherine could continue, "I'm sure we will follow some policies, Mapo, but I know we will not follow others. We will not, for instance, be part of the United Nations."

Mapo gasped and interrupted with, "What do you mean you won't be part of the U.N. world body?"

"Well, Mapo, we don't want to sign onto any existing treaties or war missions. The U.S.A., through NATO, which we will not join either, is involved in many global conflicts. If we receive a vote of confidence to set up our new nation, we will have to examine every foreign relationship from a new perspective. The Free State of Georgia does not want to embrace a group that includes such countries as Iran, North Korea, Venezuela and others that wish to harm our people and our way of life. We hope that we will link into a new union, with nations and peoples who share our love of freedom and our wish to foster a free market, capitalist economic system."

Mapo took a few paces away from Catherine, her back to her. Her camera followed her, capturing, in full color close up, her fight to overcome her rage and indignation. Mapo maintained her silence until she was sure that her audience was again focused on her, then she turned, took a deep breath, and said, "I don't want to be rude, but I think that not being part of the U.N. and your prohibition of the practice of Islam are, for most Americans, extreme and unacceptable practices, and I would never support them."

Catherine looked up at her and said, "Mapo, I understand your feelings, but you do not have children who could die in a war, one that you do not believe is protecting your homeland. When it comes to money, you do not have to worry about what you can buy and what you can't purchase. Your houses and apartments are paid for. Most of us are not in that enviable position, so national security and prosperity mean more to us than they do to such a beloved global citizen, a person who would be made welcome and comfortable in, and who could afford to live in, any of this world's capital cities. We lead simpler lives. Those of us who are mothers do not wish to sacrifice our sons and daughters on the soil of lands we cannot locate on a map, for reasons with which we do not sympathize. The flags draped over their coffins do nothing to ease the pain in our hearts. We abhor those who slaughter the innocent, and I am sure I need not remind you of the terrible attacks our people have suffered at the hands of Islamic Fundamentalist extremists."

The two women stared at one another, and the audience looked at its idol, seeing her, for the first time, in a new light. She was, it realized, not one of them, no matter how hard she worked to convince them that she was.

Mapo felt this, and fear flickered behind her eyes, along with hatred. "I'm beginning to think," she hissed, "that we should call this a Depraved New World,"

Catherine smiled at her hostess and casually remarked, "It's odd that you should say that. This endeavor has been given a lot of labels by the media, and I saw that one on a newsstand placard this morning, as we were being driven here. You must have passed the same corner."

Mapo raised an exasperated eyebrow at the audience, and Catherine ignored her and continued, "I found myself wondering, after I read it, just how I would categorize all this."

"And have you come to a decision?" Mapo asked.

"Yes," Catherine said. "Right this moment, when you repeated the insult."

"No insult intended," Mapo responded, taking a step closer and standing over her guest. "After all these years as a devoted viewer, you must know that I call it as I see it. I'm sure the audience is as eager as I am to have you share the results of your deliberations. Aren't you, people?"

Used to being manipulated by her, the audience supplied more positive than negative responses, and Mapo looked quite triumphant when she held out an airy and perfectly manicured hand, inviting Catherine to go on.

"This is what I hope our nation will be for my family and for each one of its citizens," she said, directly into the camera, "a promised land. Like the Israelites of old, the people of Georgia will shake off the shackles of slavery and walk free and tall once more. No more shall we be in bondage to the Pharaoh known as the Federal Government. That tyranny will be over, along with the constant trickling drain it imposes on our rights, our property and our income. We shall be truly a land of the free, and our future will be filled with promise."

Mapo froze until the applause died, then she said, "I don't think I care to further promulgate this evil delusion. I think it is time for me to simply thank Catherine Barton for being with us today, and state, for the record, that I am proud to be a loyal citizen of the United States of America."

With that, she turned and left.

The audience was dumbstruck. Shots of dismayed faces were broadcast worldwide, and then the cameras returned to Catherine, eager to see how she would handle the humiliation.

Mrs. John Barton settled herself more deeply into her chair, looked at the audience and heaved a sigh of relief. "Well," she said, "at last we are alone. Anyone got any good gossip?"

The roars of laughter and the applause hit the airwaves vital seconds before anyone could cut to a commercial.

John was waiting with open arms when Catherine walked off the set. "Was it okay?" She whispered as soon as his hug let her draw breath.

"More than," he told her, leading her out of the studio. "You were marvelous. What's that noise?"

"It's your phone," she said, fishing in his jacket pocket. "That's the tone I set for text messages. Hope it's the first one. You should have turned it off while we were in there." She found the phone and tapped the touch screen.

"Darned good job one of us can program the things," John said. "Wish I hadn't let you talk me into a new one. Hate getting used to them."

"Honestly, honey," she said, "it's really easy. Just give it a ch ... Good grief! John, we must go home at once."

He stopped instantly and looked down at her. "Why, sugar? What's the matter? Dirty tricks again? Kids okay? Dillon?"

"No, no, nothing like that. Jim proposed to Carolyn, and she accepted."

"Good Lord!" John said. "How wonderful. Let's forget the hotel, go straight to the airport and open champagne. Do you mind napping on the plane?"

"Won't be the first time," Catherine said. "And it probably won't be the last."

chapter

THREE

Being in Georgia in the last week or so before the bill ratifying the plebiscite came to the Senate floor was, as one reporter rather aptly put it, like living in the middle of a wasps' nest. The fact that the nest appeared to have been permeated with some particularly irritating chemical did not help matters. From border to border, in any direction, the state seethed, and hummed, and fidgeted and was, at any moment, ready to sting.

Everyone knew where they stood on the issue, and no one was anywhere near the midpoint. Georgians were either for the bill or against it, and they made no effort to hide how they felt.

Political pundits took potshots at one another, some of them so personal and below the belt that they kept a slew of lawyers busy for years, fighting the ensuing libel and slander actions. Men who were normally, at this time of the year, clustered amicably around the wood stoves and pickle barrels in country stores came to blows and broke both windows and heads. Women at church socials fought pitch battles with pineapple upside down cake and a variety of casseroles. High schools held mock votes, fought over the results and voted again. Younger kids divided into factions, based mostly on their parents' stance. Sticks and stones replaced name calling on more than occasion.

Georgians flocked to Facebook and Twitter and blog pages, arguing and cyber-yelling at one another in ANGRY UPPER CASE LETTERS. The discussions were joined and fueled by contributors from other states and nations, and they continued into the early hours of the morning. Bleary eyed citizens of Atlanta and Macon smiled wearily at one another as they passed in the rush hour, and knew what they had been up to the night before.

Brother was pitted against sister, and father against son, in a manner that had not been seen since the Civil War, and the healing was likely to take just as long as it did then, whatever the outcome. The divorce rate rose, but no one could be sure that most of those marriages were not headed for dissolution anyway. The question of independence probably just proved to be the last straw.

One of the main bones of contention was the fact that John Barton was running unopposed for the presidency of the new nation. There were those on both sides for whom this was unheard of, unacceptable and verging on a dictatorship.

John was the first to understand how they felt. Several terms in the lower house, a couple more in the senate and over a decade in the Governor's mansion had accustomed him both to elections and to seeing another name on the ballot. That was democracy at work.

But so was this, and the lack of an opponent was unavoidable. Since anyone who stood even an iota left of center refused to believe that there would ever be an independent Georgia, none of them could step forward and volunteer to be its leader.

That left the Republicans, and the theoretical possibility of a primary. Theory and reality, however, are sometimes as hard to combine as oil and water. Georgia's Republican state legislators had fought hard for their seats, many of them spending personal fortunes in support of their principals. Not one of them was willing to risk losing such a hard-won position in an effort to gain an office that might not ultimately even exist.

Well, there was actually one. Senator Harris Gordon often thought of himself, these days, as a kind of Caucasian Kamikaze. Since John did not currently hold office, his was the dubious privilege of carrying the bill. He thought he might have been more comfortable holding a high-tech, motion sensitive UXB. Harris Gordon was about to commit political suicide. Given this, there had been no reason to refuse when John Barton asked him to accept the vice-presidential nod.

To give Harris his due, he would undoubtedly have accepted anyway. He was in complete agreement with what John was trying to do and, fuss as he might, he loved a good fight. Aside from that, Harris Gordon was convinced that he and John Barton could win any race, anywhere, any time.

He was quite possibly right. Political myth avers that the tallest candidate generally gets the most votes and, in this case at least, myth seems to be founded in fact. Statistics prove it. John Barton stood at a ramrod straight six foot two, and Harris Gordon towered over him. The odds were on their side.

"Easy to see whose footing Jim's paycheck," Harris grumbled. "Look at tomorrow, John. You get a nice straight shot from Columbus to Macon to Augusta. Great places to eat in all three. Where am I headed? Up into the Appalachians, that's where. Squirrel stew for lunch."

"Look at the day after," Jim countered. "You get to spend it in Savannah. John stays here and gets crucified on the talk shows."

"Guess you're right," Harris said. "Might take Tilly with me to Savannah. She loves that city, and the people there love her."

"There's nowhere in the state more steeped in tradition," John said. "Take Dallas as well, and Carolyn, and Gallow Francis, if he can leave the office. Ask them to mingle with the crowds and listen to what's going on around them. I want to know how Savannah feels."

'Savannah is solidly behind you." John turned to see Catherine entering the lovely study at The Preserve. She perched on the arm of his chair, and he asked, "Been watching the news? New polls?"

"No," she said. "Been on the phone." She turned to address the others and explained, "I have a very elderly aunt who was named after the city of her birth, Savannah. She doesn't get out much anymore, so Savannah comes to Savannah, in a manner of speaking. She receives callers, in the old fashioned way, from two until four in the afternoon, and they flock to her door. Aunt Savannah is everyone's favorite confidante, and she is, at any given moment, in possession of more scandalous tidbits than The Weekly Tattletale ever dreamed existed."

"Better not give any of the ghouls from that rag her address," Jim said.

"Believe me, Jim darlin', I won't. Anyway, one of Aunt Savannah's callers this afternoon was the owner of a local TV station. She's known him since he was a boy. He's the one who told her that the city will vote overwhelmingly for independence. He said that Savannah has always thought of itself as a separate country, with its own laws, so it won't mind the rest of the world agreeing."

"Great news," Jim said, grinning. "No point in wasting a trip there. Harris can just stay in the mountains for an extra day."

The house at The Preserve was built to withstand the strongest storm, but its walls shook when Harris Gordon roared.

The week before Edwina Boulder was to be sworn in as America's first female president, the rather dazed looking legislators from the state of Georgia gathered on Monday morning for their first session of the year, and found the vote on the plebiscite to be the first order of business.

The majority of them, being Democrats, had never expected this to happen. They had the numbers to delay the vote until after the inauguration, and they had planned on the resultant wave of pro-Edwina emotion to aid them in defeating the bill.

Chester Knolls, the President of the Senate, had felt the same way until he received, at ten-thirty the previous Friday night, a call from a man who identified himself as David Canton, Edwina Boulder's personal attorney. Years of political infighting had made a cynic out of Chester Knolls, and the man's accent was so reminiscent of a famous political family from Massachusetts that Chester decided this was a prank and hung up the phone. It rang again ten seconds later. This time, the caller was not a man.

"This is Edwina Boulder," an unmistakable voice snapped, "and you are wasting my time. Listen to David, and don't hang up on him again. Listen and do as you are told. Got it?"

Chester barely had time to stammer out his acquiescence before the man with the Kennedy twang returned to the line and began to rattle off instructions. Chester had trouble believing what he was hearing, and he didn't sleep much that night.

Neither did the Speaker of the House, who subsequently received a similar call.

The two men met at six the next morning, at a chain restaurant off a highway exit forty miles outside Atlanta. They sat in a booth in the back, and they were glad it was still dark outside.

"She wants it ovah and done with before the inauguration," Chester said once the coffee was served.

"Ah wish this was straight Bourbon," Beecham Morse muttered, staring at his cup, "and Ah haven't touched strong liquor in thirty years. What is she doin' to us?"

"How the hell do I know," Chester said, and Beecham, who was as Baptist as they come in the Bible Belt winced. "Don't think she gives a shit. He says she'd rather start out with forty-nine states and be able to blame Neil Chamberlain than be the president who presided over the dissolution of the union."

"Makes political sense, but what about us?" Beecham whined. "We're members of her party, we campaigned for her. Does she expect us to go back to being the minority and not even go down fighting? What if there is no more legislature? We'll be unemployed. Has she thought of that?"

"Ah doubt it," Chester said. "And why would there not be a legislature, Beecham? Whatever John Barton may be, he's no Chavez, and he detests that dreadful man in Cuba as much as I do."

"Why of course he no Communist," Beecham spluttered. "but I sometimes get the feeling that, when he looks in the mirror, Governor Barton sees a band of gold around those silver locks. When you're standin' at the bottom of the ladder, it's often hard to tell if the man at the top is a despot or an absolute monarch, and it makes very little difference, anyway."

"Now you're bein' ridiculous, Beecham. No way Ah can see Georgians crowning a king."

"Why not?" Beecham asked. "They're named after one."

Chester Knolls looked exasperated and said nothing. He had always abhorred overdone flights of fancy.

"And why should we do what she wants," Beecham demanded. "If she's sure this is goin' to be an independent nation, we won't have to answer to her anyway."

"Think about it, Beecham. Try reality, just for once, instead of a plot from one of those lurid historical novels you are so fond of readin'."

Beecham Morse tried to look indignant. "Oh, come on, Beecham," Chester said. "We all know, no matter how carefully you hide them in that tooled leather Bible cover of yours. Ah would ask you to consider two points. Firstly, Edwina Boulder and John Barton appear to want the same thing. By complying with the lady's request, we please both her and the man who stands to preside over the new Georgia. You have to see that this cannot be a bad thing."

Beecham Morse was forced to nod his agreement.

"And secondly, my dear friend and colleague, we are about to find ourselves citizens of a land antithetical to our way of thinkin'. We shall be lepers wandering a sere and barren earth. Given those circumstances, who would you rather have on your side, the president of a fledgling nation the size of some piss ass European principality, or the leader of the free world?"

Beecham shrugged. "Nothin' to ponder there. She might come in handy if we need help defectin'."

"So there you have it," Chester said, laughing. "The lady is in charge, and she shall have what she desires."

"But she wants the bill passed, and a vote on the plebiscite, both in little more than a week." Beecham said. "It can't be done."

"Yes it can," Knolls countered. "She and Barton between them have seen to that. Probably the only time they'll work together, and they don't even know they're doin' it. The ballot is printed, and Barton has his people ready to staff the polling places. She's got our side lined up. Called in all her election volunteers. We pass the bill, the governor signs it the next day, he's been told to, and it goes to the people forty-eight hours later. Vote gets counted overnight, and it's done."

"What if it's close, and we need a recount?" Beecham asked.

"Weren't you listening? She says it's all over *bar* the counting?"

"And she doesn't care about that?"

"Ah have a feeling," Chester Knolls said, glaring at the little man on the other side of the table as if this were all his fault, "that she's eager to be rid of us."

Beecham Morse stared back. "Then I suppose," he said, "that we had better finish our coffee and get to work. Aint gonna be easy to get our boys to toe this line."

"Drink up," Chester agreed. "We shall need the sustenance. A great many people are goin' to hate us by the end of the day."

He was right. The two of them argued and fought their way through the weekend, on the phone, in the back rooms of bars, in living rooms, on back porches, in hurriedly opened legislative offices and in more than one car. They were exhausted when Monday morning came, but they were able to tell David Canton, when he called before dawn broke that no, there was no reason to wake Edwina, everything was under control. Each of them heaved a sigh of relief when he agreed to leave the Kraken to its rest.

The bill was called first in the Senate, and it passed after a short but heated debate, partly because three of the Democratic members left the floor rather than vote on it. The result in the lower house, a mere hour later, was much the same, and Beecham Morse rapped his gavel and lost his temper at about the same instant. "You, Senator," he screamed, pointing the gavel at Harris Gordon, who was standing in the back of the room, observing the proceedings, "are a traitor to this state and this nation! And that man," Beecham raised his arm until the gavel was aimed at John Barton, sitting in the visitor's gallery, "is your master and your partner in crime. God will punish you for this, and may He, in his mercy, spare Georgia and its people from His wrath. Pray! Pray! That is all we can do now."

The final injunction made a great headline for the next day's Atlanta Times.

Neil Chamberlain decided to save the headline for his scrapbook. America's first African American president didn't have a lot to occupy his final days in the Oval Office, so he had taken to reading newspapers from across the nation, including the funny pages. He aced most of the crosswords, with the possible exception of the New York Times, and he was becoming expert at Sudoku. For the first time, Neil Chamberlain was enjoying his job.

It wouldn't last much longer. Not the job or the enjoyment.

The day dwindled to a close, and Neil Chamberlain ate dinner with his family that evening, then wandered back to the Oval Office. His wife did not seem to have a lot to say to him at the moment, and he preferred the company of the cable corporation, so he sprawled on the sofa and watched a movie. By eleven-thirty, it was over, and the President of the United States was fast asleep.

It was by then five-thirty the next morning in Cairo, Egypt, and dawn was beginning to stain the skies. Men began to filter into Tahrir Square, the great plaza that is dominated by the Museum of Egyptian Antiquities. There, behind walls tinted the dull deep red of a dessert sunset, sleeps Tutankhamen, cradled in gold and surrounded by a whole host of other pharaohs, with the odd wife or two.

The men separated and took up stations around the square, their dun colored robes blending into the shadows. They waited patiently until cafes opened and early risers sipped their first strong, thick coffees. Traffic picked up, horses and camels mingling with automobiles, and the noise level increased. Horns sounded, riders screamed for room to pass, men shouted greetings across the square, and students from the university held noisy discussions at curbside tables. By eight o'clock, the square was crowded, and its merchants were doing their usual booming business.

A careful observer, watching from somewhere high above, would have seen that what appeared, at first glance, to be utter chaos had, in fact, an order all of its own. The students, for instance, gathered at certain cafes, each of them knowing where friends would be. They did not care who overheard their arguments, or noted their political opinions. They were young, and confident and carefree, and the women among them were treated as equals.

At other venues, clutches of older and seedier men sat at tables almost hidden by awnings and potted palms. They were just as earnest, but they had air of almost desperate commitment, and eyes that expected nothing but failure. These were the anarchists, plotting, as they had for years, to overthrow the government, any government, and seize the museum's treasures for themselves. Plotting was what they did best.

Sleek dark cars began to arrive, and from them portly bearded men in flowing robes were ushered by obsequious drivers, while burlier men with serious faces kept watch over the streets. Egypt's wealthiest magnates also drank their morning coffee in Tahrir Square. Their conversations involved the fate of billions, though they discussed only money, with little thought for the lives it would influence. They paid no attention to the government. They had no need to. They owned it.

Other men paced, usually in pairs, constantly looking around them and muttering in undertones. These were the fanatics. The religious right, striving for a return to Shariah Law and marking those who failed to observe its strictures. The female students in skirts and jeans, their hair flowing free as they conversed in public with men, horrified them, and they hissed and spat like wet cats, causing more laughter than intimidation.

The day grew warmer, and tourists began to arrive, weaving among the crowd, pointing and exclaiming over camels and robes and felt slippered feet. Cameras at the ready, they headed, in a slow and steady stream, toward the museum, whose doors were about to open.

As soon as they were unlocked, the men lurking in the shadows began to move. Some of them shed their robes, revealing business suits underneath. One pinned an identification label from a Sudanese radio station to his lapel. Another wore faded jeans and an 'Elect Edwina Boulder' t-shirt. He carried a backpack, and he was blond and blue eyed. He was Circassian, from a region in the Caucasus governed by the Russians, and his ancestors, along with many others, had fled from there and settled in Egypt during the Caucasian war, in the late eighteen hundreds. He was a dedicated Muslim, but he looked like a college student from California.

Some of the men kept their robes on, and they all merged with the crowd, taking care to stay far apart. They entered the museum one by one, passed through minimal security checks, and went their separate ways. Then, like tributaries converging inevitably to become a mighty and powerful river, they met precisely twenty minutes later on the second floor.

It was the early hours of the morning, and Washington DC was as quiet as it was ever likely to become. A tall young African American man gingerly edged open the door of the Oval Office, to find the room lit only by the television screen. On it, a man wearing a horrific mask and brandishing a chain saw was attempting to dismember a screaming young woman. The room appeared to be empty.

The young man entered and approached the sofa in front of the TV. The president was sleeping there, concealed from prying eyes by its high back.

The young man moistened his lips and murmured, "Mr. President." There was no response, and the young man was forced to repeat himself several times, in growing volume. When this failed, he reached over and touched the president's shirt sleeved arm. Neil Chamberlain spun around, leapt to his feet and covered his head with his arms. "Don't shoot," he said. "I'll do anything you want. Just don't shoot."

"Mr. President," the young man said, "it's me, Isaac. I'm sorry to disturb you, but we have a crisis."

The president slowly lowered his arms; cautiously checking his visitor's identity, then visibly relaxed and shook his head. "Forget you saw this," he said. "Confused. Dreaming. Must be that shit playing on the TV. Wasn't there when I fell asleep. Crisis?"

"Yes, sir," the aide answered, growing sorrier by the moment that he was far enough down the totem pole to have been wakened at this hour and told to brief his boss before the others arrived. "In Egypt."

"I see," Neil Chamberlain said, crossing to his desk and seating himself. "Can't be too much of one if they sent you."

"There are more senior staff members on the way, sir. I'm just supposed to fill you in before they get here."

"Then turn off the TV and go ahead."

Isaac checked his watch. "It's almost ten o'clock in Cairo," he said, picking up a remote and doing as the president had requested.

"And you woke me to tell me this?"

"No, sir, I just thought it would help if you knew it was already halfway through the morning there."

"Okay, go on."

"Well, sir, reports are still a little hazy, but it appears that a number of terrorists mingled with the crowd that entered the Museum of Egyptian Antiquities when it opened almost an hour ago. They passed the security checks, and they are presently on the second floor."

"And?" the president asked, yawning. "Can someone get me some coffee?"

Isaac called the kitchen, then resumed, "Each one of these men is wearing a bomb. Each of them is lying on, or next to, a priceless artifact, one of them being Tutankhamen's golden sarcophagus. Only their body weight is preventing the detonators from activating. If they are moved, or forced to move, they will release them and explode instantly, destroying the artifacts and most of the rest of the building, along with a great deal of Tahrir Square."

"Which has, I assume, been evacuated," the president said.

"Yes, sir, it has."

"And what do these terrorists want?"

"Well, sir, they want the government and the premier to resign, and they want strict Shariah law mandated in Egypt."

"I see," Neil Chamberlain said. "Don't they have any security in that place?"

"Yes, sir, but it seems to be outdated. Just metal detectors. This must be plastic explosive."

"Yes," the president agreed, "It must. So let me get this straight. The area has been cleared. What the Egyptians stand to lose is a building or two, and some cultural memorabilia. Guess it's up to them to decide if that's worth a new regime. Don't see what it's got to do with us."

"Oh, I think you do, sir." Five star general, Pershing Amhurst, the Chairman of the Joint Chiefs of Staff, entered the room without knocking. He was not a tall man, but he somehow managed to fill enough space for three people his size. Amhurst was the product of a military family, a graduate of West Point and a dedicated patriot.

Chamberlain looked up at the man who crossed the room and stood on the other side of his desk. He blinked and said, "I beg your pardon?"

"And you should," Amhurst barked. "You should beg this nation's pardon, and the people of Egypt's, and perhaps the whole Arab world's."

There was a discreet knock, and a White House domestic employee entered, bearing a tray of coffee. He was closely followed by Chamberlain's Chief of Staff, three members of the National Security Council and the Director of the CIA. Greetings were exchanged, the men and women poured themselves coffee and, once the man who served it had left, took seats and looked at the president. General Amhurst still stood in front of his desk.

"General," Chamberlain said, "I would remind you, with the deepest respect, that I remain, until next week, the President of the United States, and I will be treated with the deference that office deserves."

"I assure you, Mr. President," Amhurst said, "that I mean no disrespect to the office. The man who currently holds it may be another matter."

"By God, General," Chamberlain said, rising to his feet, "one more comment like that, and I shall ask you to leave."

"If I do, sir, I shall go straight to the media."

"You wouldn't do that."

"Yes, sir, at this juncture I would. And be careful when you call on my God, sir. This room has previously been occupied only by Christians, and He may prefer it that way."

"Don't we have more important issues to discuss than the president's faith," Gerald Morton, the Director of the CIA, interjected.

Amhurst rounded on him. "I can understand you not wanting to delve into it, Gerald," he said. "Damned convenient, your job coming vacant at the beginning of this administration, and you being right there to fill it. Must have pleased the two of you."

"Will someone please explain what's going on here?" Javier Vasquez, Chamberlain's brilliant, Yale educated Chief of Staff was obviously at a loss. Amhurst looked intently at him.

"You really don't know, do you? Well, at least someone around here may have some integrity."

Neil Chamberlain looked as if he was about to protest, then he shrugged, sat down and swiveled his chair until his back was to the room. Amhurst took this as permission to continue.

"The president appointed Mr. Morton here because the two of them have the same agenda. They both sympathize with the Islamic fundamentalist cause."

"I'm sorry, General, but that's ridiculous," Vasquez said. "The president and Mrs. Chamberlain are regular church goers. I should know."

"You know where he pays lip service," Amhurst responded. "You don't know what's in his heart. This started when he took office. We trained these Egyptian dissidents. *We* did. He funneled the orders through Morton, who passed them on from one department to another. Everyone just did as they were told. We're behind this."

"Behind what?" A female Security Council member asked. "Isn't this just an isolated incident?"

"No, ma'am," General Amhurst replied. "It is not. It is the beginning of an uprising aimed at overthrowing President Ibrahim El-Chahine."

"But why?" the same woman asked. "He's been our ally for thirty years. His troops fought alongside ours in the Gulf War. He's achieved peace with Israel, and he's lead his people into the modern world. What's wrong with that?"

"And he's led them away from Shariah, El-Quaida, and the fundamentalists," Amhurst said. "Our president and the Islamic Caliphate don't want that. Word that our CIA is behind this will get out. The Saudis and the Jordanians will never trust us again. The powder keg is about to explode."

There were puzzled faces, and the woman spoke for all of them. "I don't understand. Do you mean that our president has been working to empower our enemies? That's not possible. Think what it could mean for us."

"He has thought," Amhurst said. "If you doubt me, ask him to deny it."

The woman looked at him for a long moment before she turned toward the desk and tentatively asked, "Sir?"

There was no response.

Javier Vasquez stared at the back of the desk chair with dawning horror and made one last attempt to rescue the man who had been his idol. "Mr. President," he said. "What would you have us do?"

"Do?" Neil Chamberlain responded with turning around. "Do? I suggest you ask Edwina Boulder."

Javier Vasquez turned and left the room, his eyes filled with tears.

John Barton was halfway through his first cup of coffee when the phone in the kitchen at The Preserve rang. He had risen early, but Catherine was still sleeping. Knowing that the extension beside the bed would also be ringing, he answered as quickly as he could.

"John Barton here."

"Governor Barton, my name is Javier Vasquez. Do you know who I am?"

"President Chamberlain's Chief of Staff, right?"

"Yes, and probably the last person from whom you would expect to hear. Governor, I need, no, the United States needs, a few moments of your time. Maybe more. Will you listen to me?"

"Yes, of course," John said.

"There is a man standing outside your front door, Governor, with your guards. He is holding a phone that is as secure as any wireless device can be in this day and age. Will you go and take it from him, then find a private place? It will ring in three minutes."

John was seated on a bench, under a tree in Catherine's flower garden when the phone rang. He listened while he was told exactly what was happening, and no punches were pulled.

"Did you talk to Edwina?" he asked when Vasquez was done.

"Yes,"

"And what did she say?"

"She swore a lot, but she didn't come up with any suggestions. Don't think she's particularly interested in helping this administration."

"What about helping her country?" John said. "Don't bother to answer. Why did you call me?"

"Governor, I'm a lifelong Democrat but, above and beyond that, I'm an American. My parents were poor immigrants. This land gave me the chance to become what I am. I love it deeply, and I revere all it stands for. It has seemed to me, over the last few months, that you are one of the few people around who still has a grasp of what that should be. I have come to admire you, and we need help. There's a crowd of people in the Oval Office, but the president is still the president. He's doing nothing, and no one can go over his head. You now stand outside of all this. Amhurst may listen to you, and the rest of them will listen to him."

"Let me think for a minute," John said, and there was silence until he asked, "Can you get Amhurst on a conference line? I'd like you to hear this as well. Explain what's going on before you do it. I don't want to waste time accounting to him for my involvement."

A mere two minutes later, John heard, "Governor? Pershing Amhurst at your service."

"Yes, General Amhurst, and I'm proud to be speaking to such a fine officer."

"Goes both ways, Governor. Got any ideas?"

"One or two," John said. "Let's leave the Museum until last. That's a static situation as long as those suicidal monsters are left alone. Make sure they are, and we'll deal with what's going on outside. Is President El-Chahine co-operating?"

"Fully. He's a good man."

"Okay, then start with Morton. Tell him he can do as you ask, or he will be instantly arrested, tried as a traitor and, in all probability, sentenced to death. That should do it. The CIA'll know where the rest of the insurgents are gathered, and they can be rounded up. I think we may be working under a deadline here. Four or five more hours at the most, and those men in the museum will detonate. That will be the signal for the uprising. They can't lie there forever, keeping their confederates waiting. So don't delay."

"Consider it done, Governor. And what about the men in the museum? El-Chahine could well lose power if those artifacts are destroyed. The Egyptians think a lot of them."

"So does the rest of the world," John said. "I've been in that museum. It was a while back but, as far as I remember, Tut and the other pharaohs are in small rooms off the main concourse. Rooms with no windows."

"I think you're right," General Amhurst said, "but I'll check."

"Seal off the rooms," John said. "The men are probably expecting something like that, an effort to minimize the blast. They won't care, because they are just the fuse for the rest of it. Don't go any closer to them than you have to, and make sure that someone tells them what's going on, and assures them that they are in no danger of being rushed. Then make sure those seals are good and tight. Can you do that?"

"Yes, Governor. If the Egyptians don't have the equipment, we can get it to them. Might take a few hours."

"Do it in three, at the most."

"Okay. What then?"

"Just suck out the oxygen," John said.

"What?"

"Suck out the oxygen. Slowly. They'd notice gas pumping in, and detonate themselves. They won't be aware of oxygen gradually leaving, and they'll fall asleep."

"Oh, God!" Amhurst said. "That's so simple. Once they're out, we can drug them and put the bomb squad to work."

"Exactly."

"What if Chamberlain won't give the orders?"

"Oh, he will. Tell him he can either give them, and have all this sealed for fifty years, or he can be the first American President to be tried and executed, leaving a memory that will be reviled for generations to come. That should do it."

"Governor," Vasquez interrupted, "the general and me, would you have places for us in your new Georgia?"

"Any time. We vote tomorrow. Wish us luck."

"I do, Governor," General Amhurst said, "from the bottom of my heart."

And Javier Vasquez added, "Con todo mi corazon. May God bless you, Governor, for what you have just done."

"And may he save the United States," John said. "From itself."

chapter

FOUR

"I understand how you feel, Governor, and so does the President Elect, but surely you must agree that she cannot interfere with the legal democratic process in any one of the fifty states. The bill has passed, and there will be a referendum."

Beaufort Handler, the governor of Georgia, who was already red in the face, flushed to an unhealthy shade of purple and felt the blood pounding in his temples. He took a deep breath and tried to relax. He'd be damned if he'd let Barton and that ox Gordon be the death of him.

"Mizz Rivers," he said, struggling to remain calm, "Ah cannot help wonderin' why the revered leader of our party did not take steps to prevent this some time ago. Maybe, given that you are about to become her White House Chief of Staff, you can explain this to me."

"Actually, Governor," Martine Rivers purred, "the President Elect is asking for an explanation from you."

"From me?"

"Yes, sir. She would like to know how you lost control of your party and your legislature, and how you allowed this to happen."

It was a Democratic president who coined the phrase, 'the buck stops here', but Georgia's governor saw no reason why it should, in this particular instance, apply to him.

"Mah party!" he yelled. "Mah party? Mizz Boulder has worked for years to make it hers, and she's suddenly willin' to cede it to me? Darned if that makes any sense, and Ah sure as heck am not takin' the blame for this one. Where was the money to fight this? You tell me that, Mizz Chief of Staff to be. An' where was the walkin' around money for the minorities? Ah never saw any. Made it kinda hard to get any support in that sector. Couldn't turn on a TV or a radio without some ad tellin' everyone how Barton felt about it, but we acted as if it wasn't happenin'."

"But it is happening, isn't it, Governor?" Martine stated, her tone suddenly cold and filled with authority, "and the President Elect wants to know why."

"Well, then," the governor said, "Ah guess you'll just have to tell her it's because she didn't lift as much as her pretty little pinky to stop it. I heah that the lady always gets what she wants, and we wouldn't want to go settin' any nasty precedents, would we? Seems to me that we've done enough of that around heah lately."

"Would you like me to repeat that verbatim?" Martine asked.

"Yes," said the governor, his tone hard and even. "As a mattah of fact, Ah would. Ah would like you to repeat it to me right heah and now."

"I'm not sure that I can recall all of it," Martine hedged.

"Then you just fiddle with whatever device you are usin' to record this, and play it back to me."

Martine began to protest, but the governor cut her short. "Now don't you bothah denyin' that. Just do as Ah ask."

Martine did, and the governor listened intently.

"You there?" he asked when it was done.

"Yes, Governor, I am." Martine responded.

"Well, then, Mizz Martine Rivers, as soon as Ah end this call, I want you to sashay what I am told is your most shapely ass to wherever our President Elect is hidin' and tell her that Ah see it all now. Ah said it myself, an Ah was right, the lady gets what she wants, and she wanted this, didn't she? Don't you answer me, y'heah? You just tell her that I am maddah than a wet hen in January, and she hasn't heard the last of this. By God, she has not."

Georgia's governor slammed down the phone, picked it up again almost immediately and called Harris Gordon.

"So he suddenly agreed to everything," John Barton asked.

"Mmm, hmm," Harris Gordon murmured, taking a long sip of his Bourbon and Branch. "Called me out of the blue, this afternoon, and asked me to drop by his office and run things by him just once more."

"I doubt if he'd even read the agreement before you got there," Catherine said from her armchair on the opposite side of the fireplace in the study. "They were so convinced we'd go down in a ball of roaring flames that it can't have seemed worth the effort."

"She's probably right, John," Harris concurred. "I wasn't lookin' forward to the meetin', I can tell you that. I didn't want the job of negotiating this agreement with him in the first place."

"I know that, Harris," John said, "but there has to be something in place. We can't start wrangling over the details once the vote is in. We have to get on with running the country. Jim would have done it, but we thought the governor might be insulted if he were asked to deal with someone he sees as a mere staffer. At least a senator is an equal."

"Almost," Harris said. "He thought about standin' up when I walked in, but he didn't do it. He had me explain everythin' step by step. Couldn't seem to understand that we were plannin' on conductin' this like a business, with The Free States of America actin' as a holdin' company, and Georgia itself continuin' to function as usual, as an independently operatin' entity."

"How long did it take him to figure out that he could stay on as governor?" John asked.

"Not long. He's stubborn, but not dumb, and he liked that right well. Liked everythin', keepin' the original constitution for the year it'll take us to write a new one, havin' elections no more than a hundred and twenty days after the plebiscite passes, the four year presidential term, keepin' the same number of seats we have in each house right now, and makin' those four year terms, thought it all sounded great. If I'd known it would be this easy I'd have saved the fortune I've spent on Tums in the last few days."

"What happened?" Catherine asked her husband.

"I'm not sure, honey. We might as well take advantage of it, though. Did he sign the agreement, Harris?"

"He could hardly wait, even after I told him that we planned term limitations across the board" Harris said. "And he wanted me to tell you that he'd help in any way he could."

"Was that before he offered to switch parties, or afterwards?" Catherine asked.

"If he'd been a dog," Harris said when he'd stopped laughing, "he'd have turned on his back and had me rub his belly. Changin' parties should come easy after that."

John got up, went to the fireplace, slid back the screen and tossed on another massive log. "It's all taking shape," he said, his back to them. "The pieces are falling into place as easily as if they'd been well oiled. The vote's on Tuesday. Six days. A lot can happen in six days."

Peach Tree Baptist was not normally packed for the Wednesday night service, nor was the entire choir usually present, resplendent in shining white robes, with red tasseled shoulder scarves gleaming in the candlelight. This Wednesday, however, was different.

Beginning in the early hours of the morning, word had spread with the speed of an influenza epidemic. The street people knew about it before they crawled into bed and let the sun rise to at least a semblance of peace. More responsible citizens heard it before they boarded public transportation, on their way to work. Parking lot attendants whispered it to men and women as they picked up their tickets, and it spread from the basements of corporate buildings to the executive floors long before lunch loomed on the horizon. The Reverend Davis F. Jefferson had something to say, and his congregation had better be there to hear it.

There were tweets and twitters and status postings, and it was hard to find a seat in the huge church by the time the clock that towered over it struck five. Children played in the aisles while the adults picnicked where they sat, sharing cold chicken and fast food sandwiches with friends and family, and everyone wondered what was going on. No one knew.

There was nothing different about the service, except that the choir, if possible, sang even better than usual. The hymn that preceded the sermon soared to the rafters and must, surely, have risen straight from there to God's ears. Any symphony orchestra would have been proud to have Peach Tree Baptist's organist as a soloist, and even he outdid himself that night.

The applause was deafening, but it quickly died to total silence as Reverend Jefferson slowly climbed the flight of stairs that led to the towering pulpit. Once there, and with surprising strength for one so elderly, he lifted the massive bible that rested on the outspread wings of a brass eagle and held it at arms' length above his head.

"Behold," he bellowed, his magnificent bass tones reverberating around the sanctuary, "the word of the Lord."

Reverend Jefferson pivoted in a slow semicircle, the focus of all eyes, then slowly lowered the book to its resting place, leaving his right hand open upon it, and gazing down at it.

"Here," he said, "is our constant and enduring assurance that our God remains with us, guiding our lives, demanding our adherence to His laws, loving and forgiving us if we stray, but only if we repent, and dispensing His justice to those who fail to do this.

"Therefore, my brothers and sisters," the reverend went on, raising his head and staring around the room, "I have a confession to make to you. I stand before you as a sinner, and I do not repent."

There were audible gasps, horrified glances were exchanged, and the members of the black media who had been sent to cover what they had expected to be a non-event stopped downloading new apps to their iphones and began paying attention.

Ten long seconds passed before the reverend continued, "This holy book warns us against communing with spirits, yet for days now, maybe even weeks, I have walked these Atlanta streets with ghosts by my side. I have been a young man again, filled with hope and purpose. Martin has walked ahead of me, with Ralph Abernethy, Jesse Jackson, and Andrew Young, and I have followed, as I did then. Oh, I was there. I shared the dream, and I wanted to climb to the mountain top and see that Promised Land spread below me. I wanted it bad.

"Martin did not live to walk there, but I did, and all of you have walked there with me. One of our brothers sits tonight in that office on Pennsylvania Avenue, in Washington, D.C. He will leave it soon, but others will follow. Oh, you can be sure of that.

"We have found the Promised Land. We are the living proof that Martin did not just dream. He saw the future, and it is ours."

The congregation cried out its appreciation, praising God and reaching hands toward the heavens. Reverend Jefferson waited until they were done before he said, his tone heavy with grief, "At least, for a few shining moments, it *was* ours."

He tilted his head back, then, until he faced the lofty ceiling, and he cried, with all the power of his great lungs, "Martin! Do not let us fail you now!"

Then he fixed the congregation with an accusing glare and pointed at random, "Will you fail him? Or you? Or you?"

Screams of denial rent the air, but the reverend spoke over them. "Will you meekly turn and march from all that Martin strove for back into the darkness? Will you gaze, weeping, across our borders at those who still walk tall in the light, breathing free air? Will you forget Rosa Parks and shuffle once more to the back of the bus? Will you one day sit, old and feeble before your time, in a corner and explain to your grandchildren, as they wash dishes in some white man's house, why you let this happen?"

The congregants were on their feet, stamping and clapping in time to a chant of, "NO! NO! NO!"

And the reverend roared, "SIT DOWN!" Between one breath and the next, they obeyed.

"Now," Reverend Jefferson said in quieter tones, grasping each side of the lectern and leaning forward over it, "let us take a real hard look at what is happenin' in this state of ours. On Tuesday, less than a week from today, its citizens will turn out to vote. If John Barton and those who think like him prevail, we shall wake on Wednesday to find a new flag flying on the pole on top of this church, and it will not be a freedom flag. In a state that once called us niggers, we shall not be able to call anyone a racist even if they use that word, so we know that they are one. Y'a hear me, boy?

"We shall be required to produce state issued ID's before we vote, and what shall we do if the state decides not to issue that ID to people whose skins aint white? And what of our hungry, less fortunate brothers and sisters? No more food stamps for them. No more supermarkets. They'll be standin' in line at the food pantry, hopin' the supply lasts until they get to the front, and I don't see too many white folk standing there with them.

"Now some of you out there are doctors, and lawyers, and teachers, well paid professionals, doin' just fine, and I'm bettin' you're thinkin' that none of this applies to you. Think again, my brothers and sisters. What if the doors of your hospitals, and corporations, and colleges close against you? Where will you go then? Will America hold out open arms to former citizens who voted to leave that great union?

"Look around this church. Who is here to help us? Peach Tree Baptist has worked with the Democratic Party since nineteen hundred and thirty. Any election, and we saw candidates, white or black, they visited us, and we dug into our pockets, no matter how hard times were, and there was money. Money to support the just causes we believed they stood for. Where are the politicians now? I aint seen one since this whole matter of a plebiscite reared its ugly head. Have you?"

Heads were shaken, but the church remained quiet, and Davis F. Jefferson lowered his voice until it was little more than a whisper. "So we are on our own once more. We stand as unprotected as any slave, kidnapped from Africa by Arab traders and sold into bondage. We are as helpless as our shackled ancestors. Shall we bow our backs to the whip, and bend before the endless toil that turned the fruit of this land into money stained with our blood? Money that went only into a white man's pocket.

"There is no one to help us, so what can we do? We can help ourselves.

"The specter that walked ahead of me through these streets was the ghost of a man of peace, yet even he might rise in righteous rage when he realized all that we stand to lose, all that may be taken from us. Will voting against this evil bring it to an end? It may, but I doubt it. The very fact that it has come to a vote makes me doubt it. There is too much to gain on the other side.

Reverend Jefferson straightened and spread his arms wide. "It is time for us to take action. It is time for you to go home. It is time to spread the word. And it is time to make ready. At six in the morning, before the sun rises, I shall be standin' on these steps. One half hour later, I shall begin to walk. I shall not lead. I shall once more follow Martin. I shall follow him to another mountain top, or to the dark depths of my grave, and, if this is God's will, I shall lie there in peace, knowing that my voice has been raised for a righteous cause, and my blood spilled for my people's good. It is time my brothers and sisters. Will you walk with me? Will you follow Martin?"

There was no doubt that they would.

As if by mutual consent, the members of the media occupied themselves for the next hour gathering sidebar comments and stories, none of which would probably ever be used. They were then simultaneously struck by the need for food, and they adjourned to a popular soul food restaurant, where they ate and drank at an unusually leisurely pace. Back at radio and TV stations, tape editors were struck by stomach cramps, or equipment bugs, or urgent calls from home. As a result, not one account of Reverend Jefferson's sermon was filed in time for the last newscasts of the day, and the night passed without any undue incidents. The depths of the calm accurately mirrored the fury of the storm that was about to break on Atlanta.

Mellie brought the first news of it when she arrived at The Preserve earlier than usual the next morning, her husband, Mike, hovering anxiously at her side.

Mellie knocked on the door of the master bedroom, opened it just a crack and softly called, "Mistah John, Mizz Catherine, it's Mellie. Mike's here with me. There's somethin' you need to hear."

Dillon bounded to the door and pushed a damp nose through the crack, whining in pleasure at the unexpected appearance of two of his favorite people.

"What time is it?" Catherine asked, sitting up in bed.

"Around seven," Mellie said. "Why don't we take Dillon downstairs and let him out? I'll put coffee on, and you come on down. Don't you be goin' back to sleep now, Mizz Catherine. Atlanta needs Mistah John this mornin'.

The Bartons were in the kitchen less than five minutes later, Catherine in a robe, and John unshaven but fully dressed. The television was on, the sound muted, and the house phone was ringing, as were both their cells.

"Wouldn't answer them right now," Mellie said. "You need to know what's goin' on first."

John glanced at the TV. "My God, what are all those people doing?"

"That's just about every black person in Atlanta, Mistah John. They's marchin' against what you're trying to do here. It's the same in Macon, and Savannah, and just about everywhere in the state. Reverend Jefferson at Peach Tree Baptist, he preached a sermon last night and got 'em all fired up."

John shook his head, trying to clear it and absorb the situation, "Why did he do this? And why is it happening in other places?"

"We don' know for sure, Mistah John," Mike said, "but we got a call around eleven last night, tellin' us about this march and askin' us to spread the word to five people here, and five in other places in the state. We thought it was a prank, and we went right back to sleep. I got up to go to work and heard about this on the news, and we came right on over here."

John's phone rang again. He glanced at it and took the call. "Jim, what's going on?"

When he disconnected, John turned to Catherine. "You stay here," he said. "The security guards will take care of you. I'm going to the office. I'll shower there."

"What's happening?" Catherine asked. "Is it safe for you to be in the city?"

"There's a huge crowd," John said. "The city's practically at a standstill. Streets jammed, and I doubt that any of the marchers will be going to work today. Nor will anyone else. Might as well be a statewide general strike. It's peaceful so far. Let's hope it lasts. I'm going to circle the city and get to the office that way. I'll be fine."

Mike looked at Mellie, his eyebrows raised, and she nodded. "Mike's going with you," she said, speaking to John but looking at Catherine. "Black face in the car aint gonna hurt none. Might do some good."

Catherine nodded in her turn, mouthing her thanks. John started to protest, but Mike ignored him and headed for the door to the garage. John shrugged, admitting defeat, kissed his wife and Mellie and set off after him.

"Wait," Catherine said. "Here, take these." She poured French press coffee into two stainless steel travel mugs and handed them to John. He kissed her again, and left. Catherine wandered over to the sink. The wide marble sill behind it was lined with pots of herbs, and the morning sun streamed through the large window, warming them until they emitted enticing fragrances.

Catherine watched as the garage doors opened, and John's Lincoln SUV appeared. She did not move until the vehicle turned at the end of the driveway and disappeared among the trees that lined the winding road. Then she went to Mellie and encircled her with loving arms, drawing her close.

"Has it come to this?" she asked. "Must we once again be divided by the color of our skins?"

"Aint right, Mizz Catherine," Mellie said. "Never was, and never will be."

"I'm going to get dressed," Catherine said. "Let's go to Saint Mark's, you and I, and pray together."

"For all of them out there," Mellie said. "Think they're gonna need it before this day is over."

She took Catherine's hand and held it tight, and the two of them stood in the sunlight, staring at their fingers, black and white, twined together in friendship, in love, and in faith.

Rain, or a cold front moving through, might have made all the difference, might have sent the marchers scurrying for home, but the day was sunny and mild for January. By mid morning, thousands packed the streets around the State Capitol. Demonstrators were still arriving, and the crowd grew denser with each passing moment. Reverend Jefferson harangued from the Capitol steps, working his people into a frenzy.

John's office was crowded. Jim was there with Carolyn; Harris and Dallas Dee had arrived together; staffers had converged there, as had some of the other St. Mark's board members; and the media had sent along representatives to see how Georgia's putative first president would handle such a mass outpouring of negative sentiment. Jim had wanted to limit them to the reception area, but John insisted that they be allowed into the office. Thus far, they hadn't moved more than a few inches away from the long table that was laden with beverages and food.

Everyone was focused on the TV. "Those crowd barriers are going to give any moment," Jim said. "You can see pressure building. The people in front have nowhere to go but through them, and up the steps."

Harris held up his cell phone. "Governor Handler just told me he's got the National Guard in there," he said. "Don't know what'll happen if this crowd storms the building."

John stood up. "Time for me get on over there," he said.

"How you gonna do that?" Jim asked. "No way to get you through those streets, and we couldn't protect you. No way you're going."

"No way I'm not," John said. "Those people are in danger because of me. You think I'm going to sit here in safety and watch them get trampled, or worse? I want a helicopter on top of this building as fast as one can get here. Is someone going to make the call for me, or shall I do it myself?"

"No point in tryin' to stop the man when he's like this," Dallas Dee Trelawney said. "My pappy's ol' mule weren't near so ornery. I'll call. Where you wanna land, Governor?"

"There's a heliport right across the street from the Capitol," John said. "Used it all the time when I was in office. It'll be covered with people, but they'll clear it quick enough when that bird gets close. Need a good pilot, though, just in case they try to stay put and stop us from landing. Make sure there's a PA system on board. I need to be able to talk to the crowd."

"If they don't tear you to pieces first," Jim said.

"Want me to call Governor Handler and have the Guard clear a path for you?" Harris asked.

John thought for a moment, then shook his head. "No, Harris. The sight of armed troops would set this crowd off like a spark in a keg of powder. There are women down there, and some children, though God knows why. Let's try and keep it calm."

"I'm coming with you," Jim said, and so, it appeared a second later, was everyone else in the room.

"None of you are coming," John told them, "except for Mike here, if he's willing. Catherine and Mellie would like that."

Everyone stared at Mike. The man was tall, but skinny to the point of emaciation, despite all the good food his wife served him. The silver running through his black hair shimmered, and the wrinkles around them could not hide the gentle wisdom life had added to his dark brown eyes. He smiled broadly and said, "Heck, yeah, Mistah John. Always wanted a ride in one of them things."

"Morton's here," Jim said, referring to the largest of the security contingent. "Why don't you take him as well?"

"Jim," John said, "I started this. Once the vote is in, I will be these people's leader. I won't live protected from them behind bullet proof glass, or the warm bodies of others. If I am not safe with them, then I should not even attempt to govern them. Mike and I are going alone, and that's it."

Mounted police followed the last of the crowd through the streets that converged on the Capitol. Theoretically, they were there merely to observe and intercede should incidents occur. In actuality, they functioned like brooms, sweeping the people, who were afraid to turn back and face the horse's hooves, into the space around the historic building, and trapping them there.

The crowd compacted, people were shoved against one another, and some of them began to panic, fighting for air and space. A woman screamed, and the panic spread as the masses jostled pointlessly, with nowhere to go. The policemen saw what was happening and pulled their horses to the sides of the streets, yelling at the crowd and urging them to take a path to safety. No one heard them.

It was John's helicopter that saved the day. The beat of the blades grew louder as the craft descended, and the rhythmic sound provided a life saving distraction. The crowd quieted, faces upturned, watching.

John was right, and the heliport was covered with people. Most of them climbed down from the pad as soon as it became obvious that the helicopter was heading for it. A few young men stayed where they were, shaking angry fists and yelling defiance. The pilot slowed the craft until it was impossible to believe that it was still airborne and hovered lower and lower, sweeping the down tilted nose from side to side. The draft from the blades threw the young men off balance and, once it became obvious that the bird was not to be deterred from occupying its nest, they, too, descended, but they stayed close.

The crowd between the heliport and the Capitol turned its collective back on the Reverend Jefferson and waited to see what would happen next.

When the door opened, and John climbed out, followed by Mike, a deafening and hate filled roar rose up to greet him.

"Dear Lord," Catherine said, "they're going to tear him limb from limb. Someone do something. Why is he there?"

Mellie, who was sitting beside her on the sofa in the study, once more took her hand. "Look," she said, "Mike's with him. That's our men facing this crowd. They'll be fine, you wait and see."

The camera picked up the pilot, carrying the PA system over to John. He swiftly connected it, and handed John the mike. He switched it on and said, "Hello, Atlanta. Heard there was a party going on. Wondered why I hadn't been invited."

Abuse was hurled at him. Reverend Jefferson grabbed his own mike and yelled into it, repeating an old insult, "Butt out, Barton. Get yo' ass outta hear while you still can."

"Are you afraid to let me speak?" John asked. "I've listened to you on the television all morning, Reverend. All I ask for is five minutes to tell the truth. Maybe that's what you're afraid of."

"I aint afraid of nothing," Jefferson screamed, "but it seems like yo' a might scared of us. Didn't want to come without your pet Uncle Tom, huh?"

Mike lunged forward and grabbed for the microphone, fury charging the air around him with energy, and it was then that the shot rang out. The force of it swiveled Mike around, so that the last thing he saw, before darkness descended, was the shock and horror in John's eyes.

Catherine and Mellie leapt to their feet as John fell to his knees. He lifted Mike and cradled him across his knees, his head resting in the crook of one arm.

A camera zoomed in, and the world watched as John Barton's tears dripped from his cheeks and mingled with the blood that streaked the face of one of his oldest and dearest friends.

The large meeting room at Atlanta General was jammed with reporters. Microphones and cameras were all aimed at a small podium set up in front of a large banner bearing the hospital's name and logo. No one stood there.

There was an air of expectancy and a hum of chatter that stilled when a door opened, and John Barton strode to the podium. Questions were thrown at him from all directions, but he ignored them all, waiting for quiet, his face a mask of grief and outrage.

When he finally spoke, the former governor sounded subdued and serious. "My friend, Mike Newton, was shot this afternoon," he said. "The bullet that ripped into the side of his head was intended for me, and I shall have to live with that knowledge for each day of the remaining years the Lord sees fit to allot me. Mike owes his life to the dedicated staff members of this fine institution, both black and white, who have worked for the last five hours to preserve it. He is comfortable now, though still not conscious, and his wife and mine are with him, as are both our children.

"Mike will live, but there has been damage to his brain, and he will never again hear. The birdsong he loved is lost to him forever, as is the sound of his wife's voice. He has a great grandchild on the way. He will never hear the baby's cries, nor its voice as it says, for the first time, 'I love you, grampy'. Mike will now live in a world of silence, and the last sound he ever heard was the voice of hatred lashing at him and at me.

"Mike's world is silent, and his voice is also still tonight, so I will speak for him. While this wonderful human being, this beloved husband, father and friend, has been fighting for his life, people whose skin is the same color as his own have rioted through this city and others in our state. They have stolen and beaten, looted and set fires, destroyed property and injured their fellow citizens, and they have done all this in the name of equality, justice and freedom.

"I, more than anyone, am forced to ask myself why. All day, I have felt the responsibility for this situation sitting heavily on my shoulders, and I have wondered if I could bear the burden. Had I, I asked myself, endangered innocent lives in my crusade to do what I thought was best for this state and its people? All its people.

"Mike answered that question for me in the helicopter this afternoon. As we flew over our beleaguered city, on our way to the heart of the uprising, he looked at me and said, "Blaming yourself, ain't you, Governor? Well, you stop that right this minute. It aint you. It's the voice of evil, makin' a last try at killin' the good you're trying to do for all of us. Don't you let it win, now. Don't you do that."

"Mike Newton was speaking to me, but I am repeating his words to each citizen of the state of Georgia who is now out on the streets."

John stared directly into the lens of the camera in front of him, his eyes blazing now. "In Mike Newton's name I say to you, stop this, stop it right this minute. Evil is walking with you as darkness falls, and you are its tools. Like me, like Mike Newton, you want only good for yourselves and your children, so stop this. Stop it now!

"Tomorrow morning, I will stand on the steps of the Capitol. I will answer your questions, truthfully and from my heart. I will show you that the new nation I propose intends no discrimination. Instead, it is designed to be a land of greater opportunity for each and every one of its citizens, no matter what their color, faith, gender, or sexual orientation.

"I will not hide from you, nor will I stand behind bullet proof glass or a barrier of brave men. I will not wear a bullet proof vest. We are one people. Together we can build a better world for our children, but there is no place in that world for hatred. Hear me out tomorrow. After that, the decision is yours. You may make it with a gun, or with a vote. That is up to you.

"Now, like me, you must be very tired. Go home, my fellow Georgians, go home."

John Barton turned and walked away.

On the streets of Atlanta and Macon, and Savannah, and Augusta, demonstrators watched on phones connected to the web, on giant screens normally used for advertising, and in front of stores. Doors and windows, both commercial and residential, were opened, volume controls were turned high, and John's voice boomed out over the streets. Most of the television stations ended the segment by replaying the footage of Mike Newton's face, the thick blood that stained it streaked by the passage of John Barton's tears.

John's words were repeated through the crowds, and an uneasy hush gradually replaced the howls of rage. People glanced nervously at those around them, wondering what madness had possessed them all, then, one by one, began to fade away.

By midnight, Georgia's cities rested under a deep and unusual silence.

chapter

FIVE

"He seems to be rather a remarkable man."

"Yes, ma'am, I believe he is."

The Prime Minister watched the Queen, who was immersed in the early morning news broadcast and its coverage of the events in Atlanta. The quiver that had crept into her formerly firm tone since the terrorist attack on Windsor Castle saddened him. It was still there, and it probably always would be. She was confined to a wheelchair now, and growing more frail day by day. She was, after all, in her nineties, and probably missing Prince Phillip, who had been killed as he saved her life.

Without being aware that he did so, Anthony Barrington-Worley heaved a deep sigh, and the Queen glanced sharply at him. Her body might be failing her, but there was nothing wrong with her razor sharp mind. Her Majesty muted the television and reached for her wheelchair controls, turning herself to face Barrington-Worley, amazed, as she always was, by how technologically capable those of her generation had been forced to become.

She wished she had not been raised with such iron self-control, or been compelled to practice it all these years, until it had become second nature. She would like to tell this man, who seemed little more than a boy to her, how fond of him she had become, but she simply could not find the words.

He had been such a comfort since the tragedy. Throughout her mourning, her abdication, and the months that followed, there had seldom been a day when he had not spent time with her, no matter what the demands of his position. Recently, he had taken to arriving at Buckingham Palace before it was light, knowing that she would be up and alone. He watched the news with her, sipping tea, and staying until the business day began, only then leaving for his office at 10 Downing Street.

She would never forget his devotion, and she wished for a moment that she were the first Elizabeth, giving to lavishing her favorites with titles and estates. Of course, she often later ordered their execution, being a somewhat capricious lady who was easily annoyed. The second Elizabeth had better control of her temper, and no power to send anyone to meet the headsman on Tower Hill.

The Queen looked down at her heavily veined and intermittently shaky hands. So odd to see them idle. From being grimed with an auto-mechanic's oil, when she had been a girl during World War II, to handling a horse's reins with expertise, to years of leafing through state documents and shaking millions of other palms, they had led a busy life. Her days were long and boring now, and the companion who had shared them for so many years was gone.

Phillip. Oh, how she had loved him, from the first time they met as adults. Tall and blond, blue eyed and handsome, he was the only man she had ever wanted, and she grieved for him. She wondered, as she did from time to time, if he had ever loved her as much. It didn't really matter. The penniless young Greek prince had made an exemplary consort, a fine father, a delightful lover and a devoted friend. She was bereft without the sound of his voice and the touch of his hand, and she would not be sorry to lie beside him in the George VI memorial chapel at Windsor, if anyone could find room for her. It was becoming somewhat crowded in there. And she'd have to be sure to live until the restoration was complete.

The thought made Her Majesty smile, and Anthony Barrington-Worley beamed back at her. "Are you feeling better today, ma'am?"

"Better has become a relative term, Anthony, but I suppose I am. I have a dread of becoming one of those old ladies who discuss nothing but their health, so let us speak of what is troubling you."

"Me, ma'am? Nothing out of the ordinary. What can I have done to make you think that?"

"I have known twelve prime ministers in the years since my coronation," the Queen said. "Do you know that you are the only one I have ever addressed by his first name? I speak of Winston now, as we all do, but, when he was alive, it was always Mr. Churchill. I've never told anyone except

Phillip this, but he intimidated me more than a little. I was so young, and I knew so little. He, on the other hand, knew a great deal, and was most willing to communicate it. But I am rambling. I have begun to do that lately, and I do not like it. Let us return to you, Anthony. I have come to know you well, and it has not been your habit to heave sighs worthy of Eeyore at his most depressed."

Anthony Barrington-Worley laughed. He and the Queen had discovered, some time ago, that they shared a weakness for children's stories, in particular A. A. Milne's 'Winnie the Pooh', and that they both found Eeyore, the melancholy donkey, to be the most appealing character in the book.

"Ah, well," the Prime Minister said, "I shan't exactly be found, this afternoon, floating down the Thames on my back, with my arms and legs in the air, but I am a bit concerned about John Barton. I know I've told you what an enormous help he was when the terrorists struck here, not just in public, but to me as a person. I feel as if he turned me from an infantile, self-involved idiot into some semblance of an adult."

"Then he did a good a job of it," Her Majesty said. "Took Winston *and* Phillip to do it for me. It's a lot to manage on one's own, and in such a short time. I should like to meet him."

"I'm sure you will, ma'am, if he becomes the president of this new nation," the Prime Minister said. "It's the next few days that worry me, especially this next one. Someone's liable to take another shot at him, or everything he's worked so hard for could blow up in his face. Isn't it odd, ma'am? We are political opposites, he and I. I should op-pose everything he's trying to do with every fiber of my being, but it sounds so sensible, and it must be quite amazing to have the opportunity to start all over again and get it right. I don't have a problem with publicly supporting him, but I'm afraid I might do him more harm than good."

"Yes," the Queen agreed, "you might. I, on the other hand, no longer occupy any really official position. I've become a sort of museum piece."

"But a beloved one, worldwide," Barrington-Worley added.

"One likes to think so," the Queen said. "I am, after all, human, and we'd all rather be loved than despised or ridiculed.

"We owe this man a debt of gratitude," Her Majesty continued. "This country, and perhaps the whole western world after the recent events in Egypt."

Barrington-Worley looked at her and raised a quizzical eyebrow. If it can be said that queens grin, then that is what Her Majesty did. "Oh, I know, Anthony," she said. "He once again asked that his intervention not be made public. It wasn't, but ... "

"You are not exactly the public," Barrington-Worley finished for her, "and, if I may say so, very little escapes Your Majesty's notice."

The Queen nodded with a nice degree of self-satisfaction and said, "There must be something we can do to assist a man who so generously came to our aid when we were in need. Perhaps I could ... Wait, let me think for a minute. Yes. It won't take long, and it might help. Can't hurt. Not as far as I can see, at least."

The Queen's amazingly blue eyes were glowing like a girl's when she reached out and laid her hand over the Prime Minister's. "Anthony, my dear," she said, "would you be kind enough to ask my equerry to call the media and ask them to be here at, oh, shall we say three o'clock. Have him stress that he means three am. Yes, that will be nine o'clock in the morning in Atlanta. Am I right?"

The Prime Minister nodded.

"Good. That sounds perfect. The odd hour should make them all doubly curious. Can you find someone who knows a person in television there, in Atlanta I mean? That shouldn't be too difficult. Have them call my private line here. Now, it's time for you to go, Anthony. I need to rest today, and look quite regal by some ungodly hour, and that isn't as easy as it used to be."

The Queen was smiling when the Prime Minister left her, and he found that he was rather remarkably glad.

Edwina Boulder walked from her bedroom to her bathroom, where she continued to watch the news on the small TV screen that was visible, when it was on, through a uncoated section of the glass in the long mirror that backed the marble vanity counter.

She had stayed tuned to WWN throughout the night, and she had not slept much. God, she hated the early hours of the morning. Even New York City was relatively quiet, at least on the Upper East Side, and fears and doubts, neither of which Edwina would ever have admitted to entertaining, tended to come crowding in.

She had wanted John Barton to succeed, that much was true, but she had not foreseen this massive demonstration, that crucial shot, and the brilliant manner in which Barton had handled the aftermath. One state gone would not have much impact in the grand scheme of things, and she was perfectly willing for the rest of the Bible Belt to follow, but white dots on black backgrounds were beginning to dance in front of her eyes.

What if she had unwittingly pushed over the first in a long string of dominoes? A string so intertwined and convoluted that even she had not been able to see where it led. What if the rest of the nation, the one over which she was soon to preside, decided, state by state, to join this charismatic and, yes, she had to admit it, brilliant man? What if she were left President of nothing? The voice of dismal failure bleating from a deserted white house in an abandoned city that would quickly return to the swamps from which it had been wrested?

Oh, shoot! What if she just took a nice hot shower and cut the crap?

There were six shower heads, and she turned them all on, full blast. Her eyes were shut, and her hair was plastered to her head by the spray when arms encircled her and a lithe naked body was pressed against her back.

"Trouble sleeping?" Martine Rivers whispered in her ear.

"Umm, hmm," Edwina murmured, leaning back against her.

"Let me see if I can help with that."

Soft hands smoothed scented body wash from her feet to her shoulders, stroking and massaging until her knees were weak and her breath was coming in gasps. She kept her eyes shut as she was led from the shower, gently dried with a warm and fluffy towel and taken from there to her bed. The sweet oblivion she sought came to her not long after that.

Five minutes later, Edwina Boulder felt refreshed and surprisingly invigorated for one who had slept so little. She sat up and wrapped the soft sheet around her, reveling in its silken cotton as she turned to Martine, who was propped on one elbow, almond eyes wide and dark.

"This has been a wonderful few weeks," Edwina said, "but it stops as soon as we're in DC. You understand, of course."

"Of course," Martine concurred, stretching a long leg that shone in marvelous contrast to the white of the linen. "You are, as they say, the boss."

"God, you're lovely," Edwina said, caressing the leg, just as Martine had intended, "but it still has to stop."

"Whenever you want," Martine replied, her lips curving into a provocative smile. "Just let me know exactly when that is."

It was still not daylight, so the President Elect saw no reason to avoid a postponement.

The Bartons spent most of the night at the hospital. The staff shooed the younger generation away once there was no more danger, but Catherine and Mellie exchanged one of their looks, and the nurse shook her head in defeat. They drew chairs up to the bed and sat there, hand in hand.

Mike returned to consciousness at around midnight, and he was bewildered by the silence that greeted him. Mellie wept once more when she saw the fear in his eyes, and Catherine's arms were waiting to enfold her.

It was John who broke the news, holding tight to his old friend's hand. Mike wept then, and John wept with him, his mouth forming useless words of comfort without him being aware of what he was doing.

Nurses and doctors came and went, checking equipment and the patient. Brochures were provided, and they spoke reassuringly of sign language and speech therapy. Catherine asked about the possibility of one of the new middle ear implants she had read about, and was told that it was too soon to know if they would do any good.

Another half an hour passed while they looked awkwardly at one another, feeling guilty if they spoke and stupid if they did not. Mike lay quietly and watched them.

He touched Mellie's hand and gestured toward the water on his bedside table. She lifted his head, and he drank. When he was once more settled against the pillows, he took a deep breath and croaked, "Deaf. Not mute. Guess y'all were struck dumb, though."

His voice was hoarse, and oddly toneless, but the words were clear enough. They gazed at him in amazement for a moment, and then there were more tears, mixed with a lot of laughter.

"Dumb is right," Catherine said. "Why would he forget how to speak? He's been doing it for years."

Mike smiled at them, looking triumphant, then drifted back to sleep.

The Weekly Tattletale hit Atlanta's newsstands before dawn broke, and a full day before it was usually published. There were two photographs on the front page. One was of Mellie, in a crisp white apron, serving drinks to the Bartons, who sat on their porch chatting with a former Secretary of State and his blonde and rather horse-faced wife. The second was of Mike, wearing his favorite tattered overalls. He stood in The Preserve's driveway. There was a pile of autumn leaves at his feet, he was holding a rake in one hand, and with the other he was raising his cap to John Barton, who was driving by in his SUV. The headline read: 'FRIENDS OR FLUNKIES? YOU DECIDE'.

The article that followed made it sound as if John and Catherine narrowly avoided owning slaves. Very narrowly.

"Have you seen it?" David Canton asked.

"You faxed it to me."

"Yes, but have you seen it, Edwina."

"I have."

"And?"

The President Elect took her cell phone away from her ear, gazed at it in utter disgust, then returned it to its former position and said, "David, why don't you take that front page and set it on your desk. Beside it, I want you to place almost any one of the real newspapers. The ones carrying that lovely photo of Barton holding this man after he'd been shot. Then look at the two of them. Look at Barton's face. When you've done that, tell me which one you believe. No, don't bother. The answer is obvious."

Edwina Barton was able to count to three before David Canton said, "You could be right."

"I am right, and have you forgotten that I want Barton to succeed."

"In seceding?" Canton asked, and Edwina winced when she heard his high pitched giggle.

"I am tired of this game, David. I want him to become the first president of the Free State of Georgia. Is that clear enough for you?"

"Oh, God," David Canton gasped, "you're serious. I thought you were joking, or I wouldn't have bothered to ... "

Edwina Barton stiffened and sat up. "Finish the sentence, David."

"My other line, Edwina. Can't you hear it? Gotta go.

"NO! Finish the sentence, David."

She heard the chair squeak in protest as David Canton's bulk squirmed in its sagging leather seat.

"I really did, Edwina. I thought you were just saying that. I thought you wanted to confuse Billy Hutzman for some reason or other. I was surprised when the vote for the referendum passed. I thought you'd be furious, so I ... "

"No one has to try to confuse our esteemed minority leader to be," Edwina said. "Least of all me. He manages just fine all by himself. Exactly what, David, did you do when you were laboring under the delusion that you were acting in my best interests?"

"I, um, I, well, I had a little chat with a former client of mine. Child abuse case. Ten year old boy. Nasty for someone in his profession. Managed to hush it all up. Years ago, but I figured he owed me a favor."

"He? And who is *he*?"

"Man named Davis Jefferson."

"The *Reverend* Davis Jefferson?"

David Canton audibly gulped before he said, "Yes."

"And you asked him to organize this demonstration?"

David Canton really didn't have to answer. Edwina would have fired him on the spot if he hadn't been in possession of a great deal of potentially very embarrassing information. Instead, she called him every name she could think of, including a few she hadn't used since before her husband was obliging enough to drop dead.

The boardroom at St. Mark's church looked as if a group of ravenous and rampaging teenagers had partied in it all night and left the resultant mess for the grown-ups to clean. The magnificent long antique table was littered with plastic plates and cups, Styrofoam boxes, brown paper bags, notepads, pencils, cell phones, napkins, tissues and the odd sleeping head.

Dallas Dee Trelawney gazed at the chaos and sighed with satisfaction.

It hadn't been easy, but they had done it. They had mobilized the Tea Party. On buses and in vans, by plane and by train, thousands of members would be in Atlanta before nine, ready to show their support for John Barton. Dallas Dee's credit card had been used so often that she had learned the number by heart. Carolyn's plane had made a trip to the north east, stopping in several cities to pick up passengers. Young volunteers had manned a fleet of rented vehicles, filled them with supporters from adjoining cities and states, and were now all on their way back home.

"Someone better wake Gallow," Dallas said. "He needs to shower and change an' pick up his wife."

"We all need to shower and change," Dr. Mason Smith Wallace said. The distinguished African American orthopedic surgeon was slumped in a chair, sipping coffee and looking exhausted. "The rest of you are about to enjoy the fruits of our labors. I, on the other hand, need to go home and sleep. I have patients to see later, and I need some rest." The doctor hauled himself to his feet, gave Dallas a brief hug, and shook hands with Lev Bronstein and Ramon Hernandez, the church's lawyer and treasurer.

"Where did Jim Eliades get to?" He asked, looking around the room.

"I do not know," Ramon said. "A call came on his cell just a while ago, and he left with Carolyn."

"So he did," Lev agreed. "In a hurry, and looking like a Christian kid on Christmas morning."

"Speakin' of mornin'," Dallas said, "Looks as if it's gettin' a mite light out there. Time to close up shop. Like Ah said, someone's gotta wake Gallow."

Smith Wallace beat a hasty retreat. Dallas looked at Lev and Ramon, who avoided her eyes.

"I know, I know," Dallas said. "Looks like a kid, doesn't he? Hate to disturb his rest. Gotta be done. Come on, you wimps, toss ya' for it."

Ramon Hernandez lost.

Catherine was in the kitchen beating eggs when Mellie walked in. "What are you doing here?" She asked.

"He's sleeping right peaceful now, Mizz Catherine, an' I figure he needs his rest more 'n anythin'."

"So do you, Mellie. You ought to be home in bed."

"Don't notice you doin' no sleepin', and we gotta talk. Best do it now, 'n know where we stand."

"Talk? Tell me."

Mellie poured coffee, and the two women went to the table in the pretty oval conservatory that opened off the kitchen and sat down. The slate floored space was filled with flowering plants and ornate old white wicker furniture, and the rising sun sent its first rays shooting across the flower gardens and gave them the gift of its warmth.

"I plain love this spot," Mellie sighed. "Remember when you added it? Thought you'd gone crazy, but you were right. It's about perfect."

"Are you worried about Mike?" Catherine asked. "Did they tell you something new after we left?"

'No, no, Mizz Catherine. Nothin' like that. It's gonna take him a while to recover, that's what they say, 'n he' gonna need care."

"Well, of course he is," Catherine said, "and he shall have it. The best there is."

"Oh, Mizz Catherine," Mellie said, "you think we don' know that? You 'n Mistah John, you got hearts bigger 'n Texas, 'n we love you for it. Aint Mike I'm worrying about right now. It's the two of you."

"Us, Mellie? Good heavens, why?"

"Well, ya' see, Mizz Catherine, I'm gonna want to be with him while he's goin' through this 'n, if I am, who's gonna take care of you 'n Mistah John. You gonna need to find someone to do that."

"We have someone," John said, walking through the kitchen and taking a seat between them. "We have two wonderful people who do that, and we don't want to replace them."

"But, Mistah John ... "

"Will you hear me out, Mellie, and, if you don't like what I have to say, we'll discuss it some more. That okay with you two?"

Mellie glanced at Catherine, and they both nodded.

"I had a feeling this might come up," John said, "so I gave it some thought before I went to sleep. Now, there's the stables right down there. No horses since the kids left, and not likely to be. The groom's apartment's still upstairs. It'll need some work, but nothing that will take too long. So here's what I propose. You and Mike own your house, right?"

"Yes, Mistah John. Been paid for these ten years."

"Then sell it. Or hold on to it for a while 'til the market recovers. Then put the money in the bank. Move into the apartment for now. If Mike needs a wheelchair for a while, we'll build a ramp, or put one of those chair lifts on the stairs. With me so far?"

The two women nodded, and he went on, "Then we'll convert the stable. It's a big space. Make a great house for you and Mike. Once that's done, your daughter and her husband can move in upstairs. That way, we'll all be together. Louisa can help you with Mike, and you won't be able to keep Catherine from doing the same, and you can both do what you can in the house. Louisa's husband Will is a landscape gardener, right? Don't think he'll mind helping out with the grounds. How does that sound to you, Mellie?"

"Don' rightly understand it," she said. "Mike, he gets shot, 'n what do I do? I give thanks that he's alive, and that you are, too. Then I thank my Lord some more 'cause Mike can talk, 'n now I gotta thank you 'n Him for this. Couldn't bear thinkin' of being parted from you. Jesus, He says I don' have to do that no more. Bad things happen, 'n He makes good out of them. Life's just a miracle. Aint that so?"

The statue known as Miss Freedom was, as always, the first to greet the day from her perch high on the Capitol's gilded dome. Beneath her, massive Corinthian columns kept watch over Washington Street, as they had done for well over a hundred years. Trees, most of them leafless, traced lacy outlines against the blue of the early morning sky, and the statues of Georgia's political luminaries that dotted the walkways and grounds prepared to face one more day of gawping tourists and flashing cameras.

Before even the food vendors, who never missed a crowd gathering, had set up their booths, a large delivery van arrived, followed by a smaller vehicle bearing the logo of a small local TV station known for its right wing views. Several very large rectangular objects were removed from delivery van's interior, concealed in the shadows of the Capitol's entrance, and shrouded in drop cloths. Within moments, cables were run from them to the other van. They were taped to the sidewalks, the larger van departed, and two men and a woman climbed into the remaining vehicle and closed the doors. The van was moved to an inconspicuous adjacent and legal parking space, and the cables were connected. Once this was done, the satellite disk on top of the roof was raised and pointed at the heavens.

On any normal day, this might have made the Capitol Police more than a little curious, but most of them were still in a strategy meeting, planning how they would deal with the expected crowds. Before they were done, the area was teeming with people. The Tea Party members arrived first, occupying the space closest to the crowd barriers in front of the building and ensuring that John Barton would be greeted by friendly faces.

It was almost eight-thirty before the more persistent of the previous day's demonstrators filled the rest of the area. The media arrived right along with them, WWN taking the premier position it regarded as rightfully its own.

The Reverend Davis Jefferson, in regalia so colorful that it was impossible to miss, took up a position on the sidewalk in front of the building, his robed choir banked in semi-circles behind him.

The food vendors were, by then, doing brisk business.

The Capitol doors opened, and the Georgia State University band marched out and arranged itself in serried ranks around a podium that had been erected at the foot of the Capitol steps.

At exactly nine o'clock, the band began to play the state song, Hoagy Carmichael's 'Georgia on my Mind'. Before the last notes died away, the Tea Party began to chant, "Barton! Barton! Barton!" The demonstrators added screamed insults to the cacophony of sound.

Harris Gordon climbed the steps to the podium and waited until his huge bulk captured the crowd's attention and silence fell. He then introduced himself and said, "I am here for no other reason than to introduce a man I am honored to call a friend and a colleague. A man more committed to the freedom of Georgia's men and women than anyone since George Washington."

The comparison to Washington was greeted with laughter, boos, hisses, catcalls and more insults, and Harris Gordon flushed with fury. "A man," he bellowed, "who has been willing to be threatened, shot at and crucified by the media, along with his family, while he has continued, undaunted, his fight to bring all that is good to the citizens of this state. Any of you think that's funny, you see me after I climb down from here. Right now, before you do, I am proud to present Governor John Barton."

No one would have thought the crowd could produce a greater volume of sound, but it somehow managed.

Harris Gordon left, and the podium was empty for a few seconds before John Barton climbed the steps and crossed to the microphone.

It was several minutes before the Tea Party members finished displaying their devotion, and the demonstrators ran out of epithets. During that time, Jim Eliades wove his way through the closely packed bodies and leaned against the side of the TV station van, crossing his arms and watching John.

The waving signs were then lowered, and John said, "Good morning, my fellow Georgians. Before we face firmly toward the promise filled future that awaits us, let us turn once more to the past, and all that has brought us to where we stand today. Mohandas Ghandi, a man of peace and unconquerable resolution, once referred to the men who founded and fought for the birth of the United

States as, 'a small body of determined spirits who, fired by an unquenchable faith in their mission, altered the course of history'. They were, indeed, great men, and the documents they formulated created the finest and most prosperous country this world has ever known. The Declaration of Independence, The Constitution of the United States, and The Bill of Rights, can words ever have been committed to paper that so precisely define humankind's expectations and the responsibility of government to foster all that is beneficial to the people as whole? I do not think so.

"Yet these documents have a flaw. They assume that all men desire to promulgate the good of those around them, and this is not so. There are those who govern, instead, by evil, and they seek to destroy us and the freedoms we so rightly treasure. A short time ago, we laid to rest hundreds of children who, with their parents, were massacred by Islamic extremists. I know that Islam is one of the great religions of this world but, sadly, some of its adherents have chosen to use their faith as a shield for their political goals, and their leaders have been unable, or even unwilling, to identify them and expel them from the flock.

"Therefore, our new nation, with the safety of its citizens foremost in mind, will regretfully prohibit the practice of Islam until we are assured that it will be observed as the Prophet Mohammed intended: As a peaceful, loving and beautiful religion, one that acknowledges that mass murderers are not truly Moslem, and may not use that faith as a shelter for their horrendous deeds.

"Many of you took to the streets yesterday, marching in protest against The Free State of Georgia and its new constitution. You had been given, by someone you had ev-

ery right to trust, some misconceptions about that constitution and the measures it will contain."

Someone yelled, "Shut yo' mouth, Barton. The Reverend, he don' lie."

John ignored this and continued, "This must, obviously, have been the result of misinformation, and I am here
today to correct those false impressions. I am here, but I am
not working alone when it comes to the formulation of our
founding documents. We have hired the Orleans House of
London, and the Traditionalist Foundation of Washington,
D.C. to assist in the formal compilation of the new constitution. Among the instructions they have been given, the
first is primary. This national birth certificate must, above
all else, ensure that the individual is celebrated. The ideas,
dreams and aspirations of each of our citizens must reign
supreme.

"We have further directed that each segment of the
new laws sunset after the first ten years, and must be voted
upon by the legislature in order to remain in place."

"And who's gonna have the right to vote for them?"
Reverend Jefferson screamed. He signaled to the choir behind him, and they began a heartfelt rendition of 'We Shall
Overcome'. The crowd joined in, locking hands and sway-
ing in time to the music.

There was a knock on the inside of the television station van, and Jim Eliades straightened up and went to the
window. It was rolled down, and he was handed a microphone.

"May I have your attention?" Jim's amplified voice
boomed over the crowd and echoed off the walls of the

statehouse. He repeated his request, the choir stuttered to a halt, and everyone turned toward the source of the sound.

"This is Jim Eliades. Ladies and gentlemen, if you will please look to the left and right of the podium, you will see television screens being wheeled into view. Someone who was unable to be here today wishes to speak with you all."

John was as puzzled as anyone else, but he turned to face the screen on his left. It brightened and was blank for an instant before one of the world's best known faces flashed into focus.

"Good morning, Governor Barton," said Queen Elizabeth, who wore a dazzling diamond tiara, purple velvet robes and the glittering Garter insignia. "It is my grandson, the King, who should rightfully be speaking with you today but, given that I still occupied the throne when you were of such immeasurable assistance to our nation, I asked him to cede the privilege to me. He has graciously done so, giving me the opportunity to thank you personally, as well as on behalf of the people of Great Britain, for your compassion, your courage, and your dedication to the promulgation of liberty.

"Prime Minister Barrington-Worley has told me how deeply he valued your advice when Islamic terrorists struck at Windsor Castle and the London Eye. It appears that you have been, for him, the same font of strength and wisdom that Winston Churchill was for me when I was young and inexperienced. The children you comforted will never forget you. The men you worked alongside, in the attempt to rescue the living from the rubble, will hold you always in respect. The widows for whom you brought the light of hope into a landscape that was suddenly grey and ashen will remember you nightly in their prayers, and I know, for I was one of them. You have earned our nation's deepest appreciation.

"You asked, as I am told that you always do, that your participation, your wise advice, and your selfless assistance to our people in need, not be brought to public attention. I have chosen to ignore your request, feeling that such a contribution merits international recognition. I do not apologize. It is right and proper that the people of Georgia should know the caliber of the man who stands before them today.

"It is therefore my pleasure to confer upon you, in absentia at the moment and in person as soon as that can be arranged, an honorary membership in The Order of the Companions of Honor. There are only sixty-five Companions at any given time, with one of them being the monarch. This award is given for a pre-eminent contribution to the community, and you have surely merited such a description."

Her Majesty held up a beautiful gold and enamel, oval medallion, attached to a woven silk ribbon.

"Engraved around the edge," she continued, "you will find the words, 'In action faithful and in honour clear'. The poet, Alexander Pope, wrote them in praise of an eminent British statesman, but he might as well have been thinking of you.

"Governor Barton, His Majesty the King and the people of Great Britain join me in extending to you our heartfelt gratitude, and we wish the people of your new nation the joy they must surely find with one so able as their leader."

The Queen smiled as the screen faded and the University band played 'God Save the King'.

The Tea Party exploded into wild cheers. Reverend Jefferson found nothing to say, and neither did his supporters, many of whom were looking at John with a new respect. Carolyn fought her way through the crowd and threw her arms around Jim, kissing him and laughing.

John Barton turned back to the microphone, bowed his head and remained silent until the crowd stilled. "I am humbled and honored," he said, "that such a great public servant as Her Majesty, a woman who has dedicated her life to the good of her subjects, should see fit to praise what I have done and what I am trying to do. If possible, it deepens my resolution and hardens my resolve. I swear to you that I shall not rest before the task is done, before the people of Georgia are living a life that is free, and fulfilling, and fervent with promise."

The crowd began to chant, "We want our freedom! We want our freedom!" And there were no dissenting voices.

"Let us turn from my personal situation to the business of this land," John said. "I wish to reiterate some points many of you may have heard Catherine and me cover via the media. All schools will become private institutions. Each child will be issued a voucher, and it may be used at any school parents select. Yes, you will need identification in order to vote. NO! This identification will not be denied to ANY of our citizens, regardless of their faith, race, national origin, or sexual orientation. None of these will be taken into account when a child is admitted into a school, nor may an employer withhold a job based upon any of those standards or that of age. This nation, its government, and its courts will be blind when it comes to the color of your skin, the way you worship, and the partner with whom you share your life. All of that is your business, and we shall butt out of it."

There was laughter, and there were affectionate shouts of 'Barton, Butt Out'. It was no longer an epithet.

John took a moment to enjoy his own joke, then went on, "All elected officials will be subject to the same laws as the general public, before, after, and during their time in office. There will be term limits. The days of the career politician are over."

John ignored the cheers and continued, "There will be no prevailing wage to drive up the cost of public projects, and the minimum wage will have different tiers. Young and inexperienced workers will begin at a low wage, encouraging businesses to employ and train them. If unemployment is high, we will allow for a lower starting wage for all citizens. Jobs and self-respect go hand in hand.

"You will have less government, not more. Insurance companies will regulate those for whom they write policies. If you are not qualified to operate a piece of machinery, the necessary insurance will not be issued. If you run a restaurant, and you fail to maintain the health standards your insurance company mandates, your policy will be terminated and, in order to continue doing business, you will be forced to purchase a state issued liability bond.

"English will be the official language of the Free State of Georgia."

The cheers were mounting now, the crowd joined as one voice as it applauded each new pronouncement.

"Entitlement is bankrupting the United States. We must find ways to free ourselves from that yoke, while assisting the needy among us, or it will do the same for our new state. Welfare, as we have known it, will cease to exist."

There were some boos and hisses, and John responded with, "Hear me out. No one will be abandoned to suffer want. The government will stand behind private charities, and they, in turn, will assist the unemployed and the poor. They will provide jobs cooking for the elderly, in childcare, and in many other fields. Those in need will receive a check, but they will earn it, and enjoy the sense of achievement this brings. For the hungry, there will be food banks, and no one will be refused because they are last in line. Cooperative housing will replace Section 8 apartment vouchers, and all the residents will assist in the running of what will be their home.

"We will expand public health care clinics, and they will provide quality and affordable care to those who cannot afford private doctors. Many of those same doctors will volunteer at the clinics.

"We will shed the legal system that entwines us like the Kudzu. Law suits will decrease, and criminal trials will be speedily held. We will begin a national detoxification program, weaning our addicted citizens off the drugs and alcohol on which they depend. This should decrease the inmate population in our prisons.

"Even as we begin to separate from the United States, we will remain, for our own protection, part of its military system. We will, however, begin a mandatory draft. This will force our young people, both rich and poor, to interact with their fellow citizens and become an integral part of the nation. In conjunction with this, we will form our own foreign policy, and we shall not join the United Nations. We will seek to form a new international alliance with countries dedicated to a free citizenry, a free capitalist market system, and the rule of law. We will aim for the implementation of an international military tax, to be paid by all those who desire a safe and secure world. We shall no longer shoulder alone the burden of promoting peace through strength.

"'What happens,' many of you are asking, 'if none of this works? What if we enact a failed constitution?' You have a right to ask this. That is why it will be mandatory that, every twenty-five years, the constitution will be subject to a national referendum. Laws that do not work, or are no longer needed, will be corrected or removed. Our people will be engaged in their own government, and this constitution will be a living document, subject to change at the will of those it rules."

"Let me stress, once more, that the principals of individual freedom will always remain the impetus behind all that we do, and let me ask you to use two of those freedoms within the next few days. Pray, in whatever form you choose, for Mike Newton and his family, and vote for a chance to help Georgia lead the way for a troubled United States. Vote to begin our rebirth and our new 'Nation of Promise'. Vote next week for the Free States of America, and for your right to live and prosper there.

"Thank you, and may God bless you."

John said no more, and the crowd drew a collective deep breath before it began to chant, "Do it, John, do it!"

John took a long look from one side to the other. The dividing line was gone. Even the choir members were screaming at the top of their lungs. Before him stood one people, united by a common resolve. Smiling broadly, he raised his arms above his head and clasped his hands in the traditional victory pose. The resultant roar of approval carried him from the podium to his car.

Catherine was waiting at the door of The Preserve. As soon as she could, she placed her arms around him and said, with tears in her eyes, "I am so proud of you, my darlin'.

"Good speech?" He asked.

"Good?" She said. "Good? It was the best I've ever heard."

Then she kissed him.

chapter

SIX

The editorial in the London Herald read. 'FREE
STATES OF AMERICA BORN'. The article was date-
lined *Atlanta, Georgia F.S.A. (Free States of America)*, and it
was written by one Evan Pritchard.

John Barton folded the paper to a more manageable
size, leaned back in his desk chair and read, *'Here in Atlanta,
it's a lovely day for a birthday. The sun is bright, the air smells
fresh and clean, and the Free States of America have been born. It's
small right now, as newborns tend to be, and it's solely composed
of the territory formerly known as Georgia. It's a miracle, as all
births are, and many of us believed it would never see the light of
day. Yet here it is, alive and kicking, and ready to face whatever
the future holds.*

Many of my esteemed colleagues are busy wiping egg from their faces. How could this have happened? How could what appeared to be an extreme right wing pipe dream have become a reality? Surely the majority of the people do not share John Barton's conservative views? Surely, in the end, intelligent liberal policies must triumph over the whacko extremists on the other side?

Many of my colleagues believed that this was so, and the last few weeks have been filled with commentary that smirked and dripped with snide sarcasm. It was fun, but the fun ended in the early hours of this morning.

Not only Georgians, but each and every one of us woke to a different world. The plebiscite has passed, by easy margins, and, in ninety days, after elections that seem little more than a formality, former governor, John Barton, will surely be the duly elected first president of The Free States of America.

The media in the United States reacted, in their print, internet and cellular editions, with headlines such as, 'GEORGIA GOES AWOL'; 'THE UNION IS BROKEN, AND BROKE'; 'PRESIDENT BOULDER PROMISES REVENGE'; 'NEW CONFEDERACY REPLACES JEFFERSON DAVIS WITH JOHN BARTON'; and, 'OTHER STATES TO JOIN GEORGIA?'.

Setting the generally somewhat hysterical tone aside, and given yesterday's polling results, the final question can only be answered in the affirmative. Georgia will, without any doubt, be just the first state to secede from the U.S.A. There will be others, mostly, at least at first, from the so called Bible Belt. Will states less geographically connected also drift from the union? Only time can tell. Time, and the way in which this crisis, for that is what it is for the American Union, is handled by the new Boulder administration.

Yesterday's events have left the international community in a predicament of its own. Many nations depend on the all-powerful United States for financial assistance, and for defense. Biting the hand that feeds one is never a wise course of action, but what if that hand may be about to shrivel, and another, filled with glittering promises, is being extended? Which hand to take, the left or the right, that's the decision governments worldwide are facing on this day.

But does it have, at this point, to be a choice between one and the other? Perhaps the United Kingdom would be wisest to clasp the left hand in the familiar grasp of friendship, while it holds out the right to the Free States and to John Barton, extending the warmest of welcomes.

If we fail to do this, we will be left dancing with the United States, and we may soon find ourselves without a partner.

The study of history is a fascinating occupation, but it is pointless unless we learn from the past. It would be well, at this juncture, if we, as a nation, were to recall one of the past's most glaring lessons: The British, with extreme lack of foresight, did everything but support the U.S.A. at the time of its birth. Let us not make the same mistake again. It was costly enough the first time around'.

"Good heavens, John, you could suffocate under all these papers, honey, and it would take us a week to find you. Where did you get them all?"

"Jim ordered them yesterday," John said absently, still engrossed in what he was reading, "And he brought the European ones out here as soon as the plane dropped them off. He's been up all night." He looked around the room and asked, "Where is he?"

"My, my," Catherine said, "you *have* been in another world. Didn't you miss him? He came out to the kitchen for coffee over an hour ago. He sat down to drink it, and that was that. He's not up any longer."

"Let him sleep for a while," John said. "He needs it."

"And so do you."

"I feel great, honey. Don't know how it will be later, but I'm fine right now."

"Still pumping adrenaline?" she asked, reaching down to run her hand over his hair. "Might be a good thing. The barbarians are at the gate, and you're probably the only one who can stop the invasion."

"The media," John asked. "Okay, let me freshen up, and I'll give 'em a few minutes."

"Better make it a few," Catherine said. "The phones are ringing off the hook. Governors, heads of state, even the Pope, all calling to congratulate you, and they all need to be called back."

"That'll take a while."

"Yes, it will, and there's a man waiting to see you. Says his name's Rover Carlson, and Harris sent him."

"Carlson? That's great," John said. "He's a protégé of Harris', a suggestion for press secretary when Jim becomes chief of staff. Glad he's here. Okay, media, Carlson, calls, in that order. Better get on with it."

John stood up, kissed his wife on the cheek and headed for the door.

"John," Catherine softly said.

He turned to face her, and he saw that her eyes were swimming in tears, gleaming and soft, and so filled with love that they took his breath away.

"Oh, my dearest," he said, taking a step toward her.

"No," she said. "Don't come back, or it may be a while before I let you go again. I just wanted to tell you that ... " She paused, shaking her head, the words lost in the rush of emotion.

"I know, my love. I know. And I feel the same."

John and Catherine Barton stood for a few moments, lost in one another's eyes, and then he turned and left.

The wrought iron gates at the end of the driveway bristled with microphones and lenses. They poked between the bars, over to top of the dry stone wall, and from among the branches of the trees that lined the road.

The security guards stood with their backs to the commotion, arms crossed. John strolled in their direction, enjoying the crunch of the gravel under his feet, and thinking that the Brit reporter had most aptly described the morning. He wore khakis, a Tattersall shirt, with its collar open, and a soft tweed jacket he had treasured for a couple of decades. He looked every inch the country squire and, he hoped, just a tad like the leader of a new nation caught in a rare moment of leisure.

The reporters spotted him and began to scream questions long before he could discern the actual words. John waited until he was close to the gates before he nodded almost imperceptibly to one of the guards. The gates were then opened enough to let him step into the opening between them, forcing the media to retreat a step or two.

The questions were much what he expected, mostly of the 'how does it feel to win' variety, and he fielded them expertly until, just as he was being asked about his plans for the rest of the day, a reporter at the back screamed, "Aren't you as surprised as the rest of us that an arch-conservative like you could pull this off?"

John raised a hand, indicating that the reporter who had asked the first question should wait, then turned toward the voice. "Why is it," he asked, "that many of you use the word 'conservative' as an epithet, as if I should be insulted when you label me that way?"

No one had an immediate answer, so John said, "Well I am a conservative, and I am asking you, all of you, words are your business, so take a moment to look at the actual meaning of that one. You may regard it a little differently after you do."

A couple of reporters tried to interrupt and change the subject, but John ignored them. "A conservative," he said. "Or one who conserves. Why should this be an insult? Look at the synonyms in the dictionary. No, don't bother. I think I can use them for you. Should I be ashamed of a lifelong struggle to preserve the land upon which we all walk? Should I apologize for believing that government should foster and protect those it governs? Should I not wish to safeguard our way of life, to save public funds, rather than needlessly expending them, or to retain our natural resources so that they may be enjoyed for generations to come? All of these are ways of being conservative, and yet you use this as a slur. Well, I am a conservative, a conservator, or, in more modern terms, a conservationist, and I'm proud of what I am."

Before anyone could comment, John added, "Now, I have meetings to attend, phone calls to make, and a busy day ahead of me. This evening, our family and friends will gather for a private celebratory dinner here at The Preserve. Tomorrow, I shall again turn my attention to the affairs of this fledgling and most beloved new nation. Thank you, ladies and gentlemen, and may God bless the Free States of America."

The reporters tried to surge up the driveway after him, but the extra guards who had arrived once the press conference began added their weight to that of the others, and the gates were soon closed.

The next morning, the New York Times published a photo on its front page. Ramrod straight, John strode up the driveway, his back to the camera. The headline read, 'PROUD TO BE A CONSERVATIVE'.

Those who examined the picture closely might have seen that John Barton was carrying something in his right hand. A magnifying glass would reveal that it was a small flag. Like the Georgia state flag, it bore three bars, running horizontally. They were of equal width, two were red, and the center bar was shining white. In the upper right hand corner, a blue square intercepted the symmetry. It bore one, single, gleaming gold star. Above it, intricately intertwined and forming an equilateral triangle, were the gilded letters FSA.

If the reporters had listened as John walked away, instead of yelling at his retreating back, they would have heard that he was humming what he hoped would be his new nation's national anthem. It had taken a tiny rewrite and the use of only the last two verses, but English poet William Blake's glorious work, set to music by Sir Hubert Parry, still lifted any heart that heard it.

John Barton had loved the hymn for as long as he could remember, and he could think of no greater human endeavor than honoring the promises it contained.

By the time he entered the kitchen, John Barton was singing, at the top of his lungs, "Till we have built Jerusalem upon this green and pleasant land."

Two days later, when all was ready, at precisely ten o'clock in the morning, EST, the world paused. In Washington, DC, congressmen and senators sat in their respective chambers, heads bowed and hands clasped in their laps. In capital cities around the world governments gathered to bear witness. Heads of state and monarchs altered schedules and sat in front of televisions. Crowds gathered in streets and squares, partying if the time of day in their land was right for it. The Moslem fundamentalists rejoiced at what they saw as the beginning of the end of the United States.

Edwina Boulder stood alone, erect and chin tilted upwards, gazing at Old Glory as the flag fluttered in the breeze, the White House behind her, and her hand over her heart. She did not stir, and she did not speak. It was a clever move.

In Atlanta, crowds began to gather in front of the State Capitol, which was about to become the Capitol of the Free States of America, before dawn. They were orderly and almost awed, speaking in undertones and content to wait.

A canon boomed at ten o'clock, and the doors opened. John Barton walked out, Catherine at his side. Harris and

Tilly followed them. Staffers and security clustered around and behind them. The retinue walked to the dais, took their places, and turned to face the massive structure.

As Miss Freedom watched, impassive as always, The Stars and Stripes played for the last time in that place, and the flag it lauded was slowly lowered, respectfully folded and consigned to history. There was silence, broken only by bird calls and a distant siren, before the band began to play Jerusalem. After the first few majestic bars, thousands of voices were raised in song, growing in power and exultation as a new flag rose slowly until it snapped and opened, uncurling in the breeze and waving high above them, greeting the sunlight and a new day filled with hope and expectation. They cheered then, and they went on cheering.

John Barton turned to the microphone, raised his arms to encompass them all, and said, "Fellow citizens of the Free States of America ... "

The roars from the crowd drowned him out, and nothing else could be heard for the next ten minutes.

"Another great speech, gotta give him that, but I still don't get it." Parker Howell, the editor of the Weekly Tattle Tale, a publication that seldom failed to live up to its name, walked to the window of his conference room, stared down into the New York Street three stories below and asked, as if he rather expected an answer from one of the passersby, "What's he going to do next?"

"Get elected president, I imagine," David Canton said, swiveling his chair away from the television set and once more facing the long table. "And that should be a walk in the park."

"But after that?" Parker protested. "Does he know how to run a country? I sure as hell don't."

"Can't imagine you running for a bus," Canton said. "But he sure as hell can run a business, and he ran the state for years. What's the difference?"

"International relations, some diplomacy here and there, embassies, ambassadors to sit in them, that's got to cost. Where's he going to get the money?"

"'Spect he thinks he can run a country on the budget that ran the state," Canton said. "Don't think there's any law that says you have to have embassies. Maybe Zaire will let him use a coat closet in theirs."

"Do they have any?"

"Don't know. Don't care. Just meant some dumb ass country or other. Pick one. God, Parker, you're so damned literal. And you're the editor of a rag that invents most of what it prints. Makes no sense."

"Can he?" Parker asked.

"Can he what?" Canton spat, sounding every bit as exasperated as he felt.

"Run a country on Georgia's state budget?"

"Edwina doesn't think so."

"Do they have a state income tax?"

"Yeah. Edwina didn't like it when she found that out. She figured he'd have to institute one, and it wouldn't do much for his popularity. Seven brackets, and they collect an average three percent of everyone's income. He might have to raise that."

"How does she really feel about this," Parker Howell asked. "I mean, that was a great photo op, her standing on the lawn all by herself, and we'll use it on the front page this week, but how does she really feel."

"Happy as a pig in the proverbial poop," Canton said. "She wants the other lot down there to join him. Let 'em all have their own tea party, and wallow in it. Barton, he's another matter. She hates him, and she'd put him six feet under if she could get away with it."

"Bet she would," Parker commented noncommittally. "You know," he went on, turning and looking directly at Canton for the first time, "I'm surprised that you've got the time to visit us minor league players. The president's personal attorney and confidante? Shoulda thought your butt would be firmly planted in DC."

"She wants me to keep doing your legal stuff," Canton grunted. "Likes the connection, I guess."

"Don't know why," Parker said, leaving the window and taking a seat downwind from the corpulent lawyer and his ever present cigarette smoke. "We did everything we could to bring Barton down, and none of it worked."

"Integrity," Canton said. "The man reeks of it, although I'm not surprised that it took us chickens a while to recognize it. Even the Martine thing didn't do it. Still can't believe that."

Framed copies of particularly memorable Tattle Tale front pages lined the walls of the room, and both men found themselves involuntarily staring at one of them. Martine Rivers, exquisitely dressed and impossible lovely, stood in front of a microphone, a tear catching the light on one perfect cheek. The headline read, 'BARTON, THE LOVE OF HER LIFE?????'.

Canton sighed, remembering the occasion. It had, in fact, been pure brilliance. His brilliance. Martine, who had insinuated herself into the Barton presidential campaign by seeking out Jim Eliades and starting an affair with him, had quickly made herself indispensable to the candidate and his wife. She had made sure there were plenty of photos and videos of her at Barton's side, and then she abruptly left, flew to New York and called a press conference. She never actually said she'd had been intimate with Barton. Instead, she stressed her continued love and support 'no matter what has happened between us'. Draw your own conclusions, members of the media. They did, of course, and the resulting coverage was awful.

"Integrity," Canton repeated. "Can't be anything else. He and his wife, they stand up and deny it, plain and simple, and everyone believes them. Don't see any other reason why that would happen."

"What did you call this election?" Parker asked. "A walk in the park, that's it. Not too safe to walk in Central Park after dark. What if he doesn't get elected? What would happen to the Free States without him?"

David Canton raised his head and looked directly at Parker Howell for the first time. "I don't know," he said slowly. "I'd have to think about that. And maybe Edwina should, too."

There were parties all over the new land that night. Unofficial gatherings, since the pomp and ceremony were being reserved for the inaugural ball, but none the less festive for that. It would have been impossible for John and Catherine to attend them all, and he was in the midst of planning campaign strategy, selecting a cabinet and filling the various high echelon government offices. He needed to stay close to Atlanta. Harris and Tillie took the Savannah area, Jim and Carolyn headed for Macon, and Dallas and the other St. Mark's board members split up the rest. No one went early to bed.

Catherine Barton felt more invigorated than she would have thought possible when she got out of her shower the next morning, and more than ready for the busy day she had planned. She sat down at her dressing table, opening the drawer where she kept her makeup, and caught sight of herself in the mirror.

A strange sensation gripped the pit of her stomach.

How much longer would she be able to organize her own days? It had been bad enough when John was governor, but she had managed to work around that and still keep her own identity, still do the things she loved.

Was that possible for a first lady?

She doubted it. A social secretary would without question appear, and life from then on would be one long campaign season, with no end in sight.

The thought made Catherine lose her breath, and she gasped, sweat breaking out on her forehead. She leapt to her feet, her heart pounding, fighting the desire to begin pacing the room. She turned, disoriented, reaching out for support, and it was then that she saw it.

John, in total contradiction of his normal habit, had left his evening shirt on the bathroom floor. It had been carefully shaped to resemble a puffy heart, and his loosened black bow tie had been used to form the letter 'C' in its center. The empty sleeves were crossed over the letter, holding it close.

Catherine collapsed back onto her dresser stool and roared with laughter.

What was she thinking of? She would make her involvement with the reading class at the local elementary school into a first lady's literacy project. She'd visit more schools, not less. She always made time for her family, her friends, and her church, and she always would.

"Well, Lord," she said aloud, "You knew exactly what I needed when You sent me my John. He knows me better than I know myself, and he could see that I was stressed. Did You inspire him to do that? Of course you did. Thank You. Thank You."

No one, Catherine Barton decided, could take this day away from her, so she dressed and ate breakfast. Then she walked Dillon, visited Mike, checked on the renovations in the barn, spent time at the school, dropped by St. Mark's for a few minutes of meditation, ate a late lunch with Carolyn, went with her to a wedding dress fitting, picked up some groceries on the way home, put them away, chatted with Mellie for a few minutes, then remembered that she was meeting John for dinner in the city.

She was in the car and on the highway before she decided that being first lady might be a nice relaxing change.

The last of the rush hour traffic was heading in the opposite direction, so the roads were pretty clear, or what passed in Atlanta for pretty clear. Catherine let her mind wander to matters domestic. There was a birthday gift to find for one of her granddaughters, and it was about time that they had all the kids and their families out to The Preserve and spent some time together. Her two boys, both grown men now, had been wonderful about all this. Proud of their parents, and behind what they were doing, even if it meant not seeing much of them, but Ellie, their only daughter, was pregnant with her first child. She and her husband had moved from New York to Atlanta and, no matter what they said, Catherine knew that the main reason was for Ellie to be closer to her mother at this time. Her mother might as well have been on the other side of the moon. Sure, they talked on the phone almost every day, but they'd done that when they were many miles apart.

Well, there was no point in berating herself. She'd drive to Ellie and Christopher's right after church on Sunday, and spend the rest of the day there. No matter what, she'd do that.

Catherine ran through a mental list of things to do the next morning, smiled at the memory of Carolyn standing in front of her that afternoon, radiant in yards of silk the rich color of English cream, and was surprised when OnStar informed her that she had arrived at her destination.

And, miraculously, here was a parking space. Life does have its little compensations.

John, Jim and Carolyn, Dallas and Rover Carlson had all come straight from the office to the restaurant in midtown. The décor was soft, modern, and relaxing, and the drinks were cold. So far, at the end of a grueling day, no one had any complaints.

"Wonder what the food's like here," Jim said. "I booked the place because of the private dining room. Don't think it's a good time for eavesdroppers to pick up snippets of conversation and put their own slant on them. Anyone eaten here before?"

"Says its contemporary Southern," Dallas Dee commented, peering suspiciously at the menu cover. "Darned good thing, if you ask me. Never had much of a hankerin' for antique food."

They were all laughing when a server ushered Catherine in. John rose and went to greet her, briefly holding her close and kissing her cheek. He seated her next to him, took her hand and said, "Think you know everyone, darlin'."

'Yes," she said. "Hi, y'all. I even met Mr. Carlson when he came to the house this morning. Nice to have you onboard," she added, smiling at the young man who sat at the opposite end of the table, looking a little lost. "May I call you Rover?"

The fair haired and blue eyed, tall and gangly thirty year old took the full brunt of that smile and blushed from his collar to his hairline. "Yes, ma'am, Mrs. Barton, I'd be honored if you'd do that," he stammered. "Know it sounds like some Brit name for a dog, but it's a family name, and we're proud of it."

"I'm sure you are," Catherine said. "And you should be. Family is most important but, if I am to call you Rover, you must call me Catherine, and forget the 'ma'am'. You'll be with us so much that we shall be like family, too."

"I'll do that, ma'am ... er ... Catherine," Rover said, reaching for his water and gulping down half the glass.

"Thank you, and will you try and spend a little time with me tomorrow and tell me about yourself?"

"Yes, Catherine, I'd like that," Rover said, smiling back at her, the pink slowly fading from his face.

"Good, I shall look forward to it. Now, Mr. Eliades, sir, tell me what has been going on all day in what I hope were not smoke filled rooms. I shall get a more accurate report from you than I shall from this husband of mine, who will try to make it seem as if this entire campaign will involve little more than a couple of Sunday afternoon jaunts around the Atlanta countryside."

There was more laughter, a server knocked and entered, and orders were placed from what looked to be a delicious and different menu. Dallas found a steak, and ordered it 'mooing'.

By the time the food was served, Catherine had been informed that John wanted to schedule speaking appearances with religious and business groups, service clubs, VFW's and American Legion groups, teachers and other union members, conservatives and liberals, across the state.

"Sounds to me like he'll have chronic laryngitis by the end of next week," Dallas growled. "An' I'm danged if I know why he's botherin' with them pesky liberals."

"Dallas, Dallas, Dallas," John said. "If I'm to be president, then I'm to be everyone's leader, not just a figurehead for the people who think I'm right when they get out of bed in the morning. I need to know what all the people want from this new nation, no matter what side of the party line they stand on. When it boils down to it, they still want what's best for them and their kids. That's what we all want."

"And you think you can persuade them that you know how to get it for them," Carolyn McKay asked.

"I think the time for persuading is passed, Carolyn," John said. "The Free States is a reality, and what I want is for us all to find a way to work together. I don't expect a total lack of opposition, but what I don't want is a fractured legislature behaving the way that bunch in DC acted throughout the Chamberlain administration. Thinking of the good of their parties, not the good of the people. Nothing gets done that way, we all saw that."

There were nods of agreement, and Catherine asked, "Any cabinet decisions?"

"Feel strange making them before I'm elected," John said, "but it has to done, I guess. I want people I know and trust around me, so I've asked Ramon to take a position over at Treasury. Not comptroller, he'll stay on, but in a sort of ombudsman post that will let him keep an eye on things for me."

"Won't be easy for him," Jim put in. "They'll know why he's there, and they'll resent him and wonder why the treasurer of a church is qualified to have anything to do with them."

"Castro couldn't intimidate Ramon Hernandez," John said. "So I don't think a pack of southern bureaucrats stand much of a chance. And he ran a thriving business in Cuba, lost it to the revolution, came here penniless, started another and made it a huge success. I'll make you a level bet that at least thirty people in this restaurant, right now, are wearing shoes Ramon's company made. I'd say he knows how to manage money, and this nation is just a business on a larger scale. Not entitled to run up massive debt just because we call ourselves a country, not a corporation."

"I can't argue with that," Catherine said, "and I think it's a good idea. Anything else I need to know before the food arrives and I stop listening. I'm starving."

"The Attorney General stays. Lev Bronstein becomes my personal liaison to that office. We tried to persuade Mason Smith Wallace to take Health and Human Services, but he won't leave his patients. Says he'll be an advisor. We'll put Peter Havin, over at Georgia General, to work on it. He'll find the right man or woman for us."

"And we thought that was enough decisions for one day," Jim interjected. "We can tackle the rest of the posts one by one. Set up search committees of experts from each field. We have to concentrate on the election. That's first and foremost."

Catherine looked at him intently. "We've known one another for a lot of years now," she said. "Can't count the campaigns. Don't want to. I've never seen you this intense, Jim. Shouldn't this be the easiest one of all? Why are you so worried about it? There isn't even another name on the ballot."

Jim shook his head, heaved a sigh, and ran his fingers through his hair. "Wish I knew, Catherine. Just seems to me that there's so much at stake. Look what this husband of yours has done. He's broken the Union. We're out here, on our own, trying to find a place in this crazy world for this country and its people. Sounds like I'm putting the full responsibility on John's shoulders, and I am. It wouldn't have happened without him, and without him as its leader, the country faces nothing but chaos for a lot of years to come. That, or crawling to Uncle Sam and begging to be allowed back inside the fence. It all boils down to this man," he said, holding out a hand toward John, "and I'm the one who has to put him in office. If I fail, history will be irrevocably altered. Not a great prescription for a good night's sleep!"

President Edwina Boulder did not occupy the master bedroom suite on the second floor of the White House, where the family quarters are located. She'd slept there with another president, with the same last name, and she did not relish the recollection.

When asked to select one of the other bedrooms, she had revisited the two suites at the east end of the floor. They each opened off the so called 'sitting hall' there. She'd never much cared for the Queen's Bedroom, finding it too pink. The adjacent sitting room was too blue, and there was some sort of wicker construction over the toilet in the bathroom that looked as if it might scratch tender flesh at the slightest provocation.

Now, the Lincoln Bedroom that was another matter. The bed was vast, and the entire room was a monument to Victorian opulence. It was fit for a Czar and, thus, fit for Edwina Boulder.

She'd had a nice quiet dinner with Minority Leader, Billy Hutzman. Meat loaf, jeans and an old sweatshirt. Who could ask for more? She was so damned sick of dressing up all the time. She'd taken a long bath in the large tub, which was etched with a presidential eagle. "Presidential, my ass!" she had thought as she slid down over it, and her laughter had echoed off the mirrored dome ceiling light.

The president was now ready for bed. The covers were turned back, and a nice selection of New York Times best sellers was on the night stand. Edwina sighed with pleasure as she settled in with one of the books.

And the phone rang.

She debated ignoring it, but some jerk might have decided to set another fire in Chicago, so she picked it up.

"Yes?"

"Madame President, this is Martine. David Canton is in my office. He has something to say, and I think you should hear it."

chapter

SEVEN

"I've bought a house," Carolyn said once she and Jim were alone in the car, on their way home.

"A house," Jim echoed. "You want to move?"

"No, sweetheart, I grew up in my house, and I love it. Aside from that, if it was a home for the two of us, we wouldn't buy unless you loved it, too. Oh," she suddenly said, turning to look at him, his profile outlined by the lights from passing cars, "I never thought to ask. How dreadful of me. Do you hate my house? Would you like to live somewhere else? I really wouldn't mind if you did."

"As far as I know, and I'm pretty sure I'm right," Jim said, setting his hand on her thigh and gently squeezing, "that's the first lie you've ever told me, my lady. Don't let it become a habit."

"It's not really a lie," Carolyn said. "I do love the house, and I'd never sell it. How nice to know that I don't have to, but I'd live anywhere you wanted. You know that."

"And I want to live in your home, with you," Jim said, "and make it ours, which brings us back to the beginning of this. Why have you bought a house?"

"It's not easy to explain," Carolyn said, "and I wouldn't even expect anyone else to really understand, but I think you will."

"Do my best," Jim said, pulling onto the highway. "Go ahead."

Carolyn shifted in her seat, so that she could see him without twisting her neck, and said, "I think it all started with the wedding guest list."

"Carolyn," Jim protested, "I know money's not an issue, but you can't start giving out houses as party favors. It's pretentious, and expensive."

"Even if I kept them under three thousand square?" she asked, exuding innocence. "Stop kidding. This is serious, darling."

"Sorry, sweetheart," Jim said. "Couldn't resist. Not used to life in the financial stratosphere. I'm all ears. Serious ears. Go ahead."

"It was your family," Carolyn said. "There are so many of them, and that's lovely. Your side of the list was yards long, even before you started on friends and the political people."

"That's what Greeks do," Jim said, "we have families, and most of the others would be on your list, too."

"I know," Carolyn began, "but ... "

Before she could finish the sentence, she became aware of movement close beside them. She glanced at Jim's window in time to see headlights heading straight for them. Carolyn would always remember the sound of the impact more than the sensation, and the car began a crazy sideways dance across the highway. Their seatbelts locked, and Jim's sunglasses flew from the dashboard, catching a glancing blow on Carolyn's cheek before they disappeared into the darkness behind her. The airbags exploded, and the fumes filled the car. Tires and brakes squealed as other drivers swerved to avoid them. In seconds, the central barrier loomed in front of them. Carolyn screamed as the car began to climb the concrete wall.

Jim fought the wheel, knowing that plummeting over the barrier into the traffic on the other side would mean their death, and that they would probably take others with them. There was a sickening moment when the car seemed to be deciding between rocketing into the northbound lanes, or falling onto its back in front of the oncoming traffic. For Jim, it was all happening in slow motion. He seemed to have so much time to make choices, and mentally compute their results. He could hear nothing but the engine and the sound of steel scraping against the barrier, and he prayed that Carolyn was okay. Then he applied gentle pressure to the wheel and turned it a smidgen to the right. Almost reluctantly, the car slid down the barrier, hitting it once more with its rear end, which sent them careening across the highway again.

Jim heard another collision behind him, and then another, and then, somehow, they came to a halt. The car was still running, and he was able to pull it onto the hard shoulder.

"Carolyn?" It was almost a scream. "Carolyn."

"I'm okay," she said. "At least I think I am. I was just too frightened to make a sound. Get me out of this car. Please get me out."

Jim was out of his door in less than a heartbeat. He ran around, threw hers open, and found her fumbling with her seatbelt. He undid it for her, pulled her into his arms, and half carried her to the railing, seating her on it.

"Are you really all right," he asked. "Does anything hurt?"

"No," she said, "but my legs are shaking, and I'm not sure I can stand up. Not good. I want to be in your arms."

He lifted her and held her, his face buried in her neck. "Oh, dear God," he said, "thank You. How would I have lived if I had lost her?"

They were still standing there, clinging to one another, when the police cars and the ambulances arrived.

It was almost four hours before they crawled into bed. They had been taken to the hospital and checked out. After being poked, and pummeled and x-rayed, all of which seemed to take forever, Carolyn was told that she had sustained nothing more than some bruises, including a small one on her cheek, where the sunglasses had hit her, and a burn across her neck, caused by friction from the seatbelt. The doctor said that it often happened to small people, and assured her, over and over again, that Jim was bruised and had pulled muscles, wrestling with the car. He would be sore for a few days, but fine after that. She was asked if she felt well enough to give a statement to the police, and the doctor nodded when she said that she did. "You are both very lucky," he'd said as he left the room.

Carolyn and Jim had no problem with a little luck, but they visited the hospital chapel before they saw the police, and they held hands as they gave thanks.

The officers who took their statements had seen the skid marks on the road, and the damage to Jim's car, and even they seemed amazed that neither of them was seriously injured. The other collisions, they were glad to hear, had been minor. The driver who hit them had left the scene. The police estimated that the vehicle was something large, most likely an SUV, travelling at over ninety miles an hour. "Doubt that the driver was sober," one of the officers had commented.

"Don't think this bed ever felt so wonderful," Carolyn said, snuggling into the pillows. "Are you in any pain, my love?"

"No," Jim said, "although I expect that I shall be sore in the morning. Speaking of which, I'm going to text John and tell him we're okay, just in case this makes the early news."

"Good idea," she said. "Then we can sleep."

"Not so fast, lady! You still have a question to answer.

"I do?"

"Yes. House?"

"Oh, that. I'd almost forgotten about that."

"You rich kids, you're all the same," Jim said, pressing 'send' and connecting his phone to the charger on the bedside table. "A few hundred thousand here, a few hundred thousand there, it means nothing to you."

"On the contrary, sir," she said, "this means a lot to me and, if you'll lie down, I'll tell you."

Jim was more than happy to concur, and Carolyn's head was resting on his shoulder before she said, "We dealt with your guest list, right? So, then, I got to mine, and it started with John and Catherine. I love them so much, but it was the first time I had ever really realized that I have no family."

"You have me," Jim said, "and we'll make our own family."

"I know, darling, and that's wonderful but, you see, there was no one coming to my wedding just for me, because they loved me, and I was their family, and that's why I bought the house."

"Did it come with a family?"

"No, idiot," she said, cuffing him lightly, "it did not. As a matter of fact, it didn't even come with a washer and dryer."

"So you need people to live in it who don't mind dirty clothes?"

"Yes," Carolyn said, "I suppose you're right about that, and the people I'm thinking of are grateful for any clothes they can get. God, I wonder what that doctor gave me. All I want to do is sleep."

"Not before you explain," Jim said, "and it is after three in the morning."

"My children," she said. "I love all of them, but there are five, from four different countries, whose faces never leave my mind. I see their eyes and their smiles, and I feel their arms around my neck when I fall asleep, and when I wake up. They are all orphans, victims of war, and they are all in camps."

"And they are your family," Jim said, holding her close. "Our family."

"Yes," Carolyn said. "I have talked to the state department, and we are working on bringing each of them here. They have been injured, both their tiny bodies and their minds. Jehan has one leg, and M'boto is blind. Starvation leaves lingering problems that must be dealt with. My kids are political refugees. I shall be their sponsor, and they will live in this house, with all the care they need, until they are well and all the paperwork is done."

"And then," Jim said, "they will come home, and other kids will take their places, and you will find good homes for them all."

"Ah," she sighed. "You do understand, and I love you so much."

"God," he said, kissing her cheek, "took care of precious cargo tonight. More precious than even I knew."

Carolyn did not reply, and Jim fell asleep in the fragrant cloud of her hair.

Being dragged out of bed had not made President Boulder happy, and listening to David Canton had not improved her mood.

"I would have liked to get beyond the first two sentences," she remarked as soon as he stopped speaking.

"I'm sorry?"

"Of the book I was reading before you interrupted me, Martine. Did I really have to get out of bed, on the first free evening I've had for months, to listen to David state the obvious? Couldn't it have waited until morning? He could then have added that it was Wednesday, and I would have felt truly fully informed."

"Thought you might like to be the president who re-formed the union," Canton said.

"Lincoln already did that. It's kinda lost some of its impact over the years, and I don't want to reform the union. Just how often do I have to say this before it sinks in?"

"But take out Barton, and ... "

"We can't take out Barton, David," Edwina interjected. "Lord knows we tried hard enough, and where did it get us."

"But supposing he had an accident."

Edwina leapt to her feet. "I am the president of the United States. I will not discuss 'accidents' that might occur in the lives of other political figures with you or anyone else."

"Except, perhaps, the head of the CIA."

"Oh, funny, David. Very funny. I am going back to bed, and I suggest that you occupy yourself elsewhere until I decide that I can bear to look at you at least once more."

The threat was implicit, and David Canton instantly ran a mental check of his bank balance, wondering if it could survive a long unemployment. Edwina would make sure that it was long, and it was probably a bit late to throw himself on the mercy of the GOP. Nah! She could never do it. He had too many files, and he kept them all very safe.

"Not quite safe enough, David," Edwina said, as if he had spoken out loud. "Haven't you checked lately? Maybe you should. I burned them all myself. It took a while. I'd never realized what a careful record keeper you are, and you hid them well. It took the FBI three days to find them. Three whole days. Think of what you cost the taxpayers, David. That should make you proud. Now, get out."

David Canton has almost reached the door when the phone rang.

"Who the hell is that," Edwina asked. "Don't these people ever sleep?"

Martine answered the call, and listened for a few seconds, saying nothing except, "Yes, Ma'am." She then handed the phone to Edwina. "It's the Secretary of State."

"Oh, well," Edwina said, "might have known it was her. She never sleeps, mostly because she can't find anyone to sleep with her."

"Not an accurate statement, Edwina," Cornelia Oats said, "but we can discuss that at a later date. Right now we have an international crisis on our hands. Your first one. Think you're ready for it?"

"What's going on?" Edwina asked, marching into the Oval Office and seating herself behind her desk. Martine stationed herself in doorway, ready to take any action necessary, and David Canton joined her.

"Mumbai has been hit by a missile," the Secretary of State announced. "It would seem that it could only have been launched from Pakistan, and it was directed at the center of the commercial district. We have, as yet, no accurate death toll, but it will be in the thousands."

"What time is it there?"

"It's the middle of the morning, Madam President. The attack was timed so that the maximum number of people would be in the workplace."

"Give me a reason," Edwina said, "why Pakistan would attack India without any warning."

"There isn't an apparent one," Ms. Oats told her. "There's always Kashmir, of course. They've never been able to decide which of them owns that, but there's been no indication, on either side, that that situation was deteriorating. You need to speak to Prime Minister Achari as soon as possible."

"Martine," Edwina said, "get the security advisors in here stat. Pakistan's a Moslem nation. They could have other plans in the works."

Martine and David disappeared, and Edwina used a remote to tune several TV's to different news stations, muting the sound. "You call him, Cornelia," she said. "Tell him I'll speak to him as soon as I've met with my advisors. Is he thinking of retaliation? That could be a disaster."

"I think I can get him to wait until he speaks to you," the Secretary of State said. "We worked on the same committee once, when I was with the World Bank, and we got on well. He trusts me."

"Does he indeed?" Edwina said. "It'll take the crew a few minutes to get here. Update me on Mumbai while I wait."

"It'll be short and snappy, Madam President. I need to make that call."

"Well I am short and snappy," Edwina responded, "so go ahead."

"Mumbai was formerly known as Bombay. It is densely populated; it is India's business and entertainment capital, and one of the world's largest centers of commerce. It has a flourishing port, and large numbers of computer tech support services are headquartered there, along with a great many financial institutions. The majority of the population works for the government. Some of India's premier scientific and nuclear institutes are there, along with movie and TV studios. Enough?"

"Sounds like a page from Wikipedia," Edwina said.

"And that could be where my staff found it, ma'am."

"Thought we did our own research."

"This *was* a rush job, and I could have been joking."

"Joking? Not you, Cornelia. You know, I don't like you any more than you like me, never have. I wonder why I gave you this job."

"You needed another woman on the cabinet," Cornelia said. "Can't have our first female president being accused of gender bias, can we. I have to make that call now."

Edwina broke the connection without saying another word.

"Dear Lord," Catherine gasped, staring at the photo on Jim's phone. "You can barely tell it's a car. How did the two of you survive this, let alone basically uninjured?"

"It was a minor miracle," Jim said.

"Minor? This is more than minor, and the other driver was drunk?"

"No way to really know," Carolyn told her. "He drove away, but the police said it was more likely than not."

Catherine went to her and hugged her gently. "It was so kind of you to come over. I'm sure you didn't feel like getting up early, but I'd never have believed this if I hadn't seen it with my own eyes. I'd have thought the two of you were minimizing things, so I wouldn't worry."

"I don't see how anyone could drive away from that mess," Carolyn said. "How could you live with the thought that you had hurt someone and done nothing about it?"

"He was scared of a DUI," Jim said.

"Then why do people drink and drive?" Carolyn asked. "Harming yourself is one thing, if you want to be crazy enough to do it, but risking harming others? That's incomprehensible. There ought to be cabs, lots of them, and cheap, so that anyone who's been drinking can get home safely."

"And bartenders should be able to ask for your car keys after the third drink," Catherine added. "Then they could give them to the cab driver, who'd return them to you when you paid."

"You're right, Catherine," Carolyn said. "And it should just be the way it's done, so everyone accepts it. No one's saying you're drunk, but if you want another, give me the keys, and I'll call a cab when you're ready."

"That's a damned good idea," Jim said. "I'm gonna talk to John about that. Do a state-wide program. Make it routine. You drink or get high, this is the way you go home. Might help with the macho thing. You know, the guy who's convinced he can drive when he can barely stand. Taking his car keys is tantamount to castrating him. Better to get them when he's still relatively sober. I have to get to the office. Will you be okay, sweetheart?"

"She'll be better than that," Catherine said. "She is going straight to the study for a nice long nap, followed by an even nicer lunch."

"You must believe me, Madam President. Neither I nor the Prime Minister, who is here with me, had any knowledge of this attack."

Tariq Khan, the president of Pakistan, was sweating despite the air conditioning in his office.

"I do, Mr. President," Edwina Boulder said, "but a rogue attack could be even more of threat to international security. None of us has any way of telling what will happen next. Do you have any idea who might be responsible?"

"Would it be offensive to you, Madam President, if I put this call on the speaker? I assure you that no one else, except the prime minister, is in the room."

"Go ahead, Mr. President. Good afternoon, Prime Minister Malik."

"Madam President," Raheem Malik said in British accented English, "I am sorry that we should speak for the first time under such tragic circumstances. Thousands of India's citizens are dead, the property damage is inestimable, and we have no idea how this happened. I agree with the Prime Minster that the most likely suspects are the I.S.I, or a military splinter group that has put itself beyond governmental control, or both. We suspect a particular General, and he has been arrested. There is, sadly, no doubt that the missile was one of ours."

"I.S.I, isn't that your Inter Service Intelligence agency, and didn't they work closely with our CIA in Afghanistan and after the 9/11 attack?"

"Yes, ma'am, you are right on both counts, but we believe that the agency may have been infiltrated by Islamic extremists. Our new recruits are young and impressionable, and all faithful servants of Allah. It is not hard to sway enthusiastic and immature minds if one is determined to do so."

"Do they have access to more missiles?" Edwina asked.

"We are doing a full count," Tariq Khan told her. "So far, we have not found any discrepancies."

"There is one other matter we feel we must mention, ma'am, Raheem Malik said. "Mumbai is the site of the Atomic Energy Establishment, India's prime nuclear research center. They have active nuclear reactors there, for research purposes. The reactors are, supposedly, impervious to missile attacks, though this has, of course, never actually been tested. The center sustained only minor damage, but we cannot be sure if this was good fortune, or if the missile was supposed to strike there, and someone made a miscalculation."

"I see," Edwina said. "Are you expecting more attacks on India, or attacks on other countries, for that matter, such as my own?"

"We are caught in a quandary, ma'am," the President of Pakistan said, leaning over the phone and shaking his head, as if Edwina could see him. "The safest course for us to take," for India's protection, if not for the world's, would be to lock down our bases, ground our planes, and order our navy into port. This way, we could take a full roll call, both in the military itself, and in the military intelligence services, and we would know if anyone is missing."

"But there is a catch to this, Madam President," Malik added. "If India retaliates, as she has a complete moral right to do, we will need our armed forces both to protect our people, and to deal with the aftermath of the attack. We must know what President Achari is going to do. I cannot stress how vital this is."

"And all of us are vulnerable until then," Edwina said. "We are in Aadil Achari's hands. I'll speak to him, and get back to you."

He liked to think of himself as a man of peace. An academic, with a father who revered Gandhi, he grew to maturity with the Mahatma's example always before him. A life-long Hindu, he had also realized, at some point in his early university career, that Gandhi's influence crossed national and religious boundaries. Hadn't Martin Luther King said, 'Christ gave us the goals, and Mahatma Gandhi the tactics'? Non-violence was the axis around which his personal philosophy, and all that he did, revolved.

And, right at this moment, Aadil Achari was angry enough to launch his nation's entire arsenal and obliterate the fiends who had wreaked this havoc.

He had been flown from New Delhi to a military base outside Mumbai. From there, a helicopter took him to the disaster area, and hovered above it. Despite many protests, he insisted that it land, and he stepped out into hell.

It was difficult to imagine that this had ever been the commercial heart of a city that filled India with pride; a city that stood as a constant testament to the country's role in modern technology, and in the world's financial markets.

There was very little debris in crater itself. The explosion had seen to that. Around the rim, jagged metal was all that remained of banks and corporations, restaurants and towering office buildings.

There were bits of bodies. That was all.

It was a few minutes before Aadil Achari could move, or even hear. After that, the world came rushing in. He felt as if he were drowning in the shouts of the emergency teams, the roar of machinery, the sound of women wailing and, over it all, an infant's shrill cry. It was hard to breathe.

Aadil Achari spent an hour with his stricken people before he returned to the base.

He was now once more on the plane, fighting the urge to order a massive strike, one that would bring death and destruction to hundreds of thousands, all of whom would be innocent.

Aadil Achari wished that he could care about that.

An aide approached and told him that Edwina Boulder was calling, and wished to speak to him. Aadil Achari wished only to speak to his generals, but one does not ignore a call from the President of the United States.

"Madam President, this is Aadil Achari."

Edwina first conveyed the conventional condolences, then related her conversation with Pakistan's Premier and

Prime Minister. It wasn't easy to ask the final question. There was no tactful way to put it.

"What am I going to do?" Aadil Achari repeated. "To be frank, I do not know. I have just left Mumbai, and I am filled with an emotion foreign to me. I want revenge."

Edwina ended the call ten minutes later. India's premier had urged her to begin a United Nations investigation into the attack. That was good. Pakistan wanted the same thing. What he had not done was commit to non-retaliation, so the most powerful woman in the world was going to have to eat some crow. Failure is very bad for the digestion.

Aadil Achari was given only moments to grapple with his dilemma before Anthony Barrington-Worley called. He conveyed his personal sympathy, his nation's, and his monarch's. He stressed that the Dowager Queen retained, in her heart, a special place for the people of India, so many of whom lived in Great Britain, and all of whom had regarded her father as their King and Emperor.

After that, he asked the same question. When he received the same answer, the Prime Minister hesitated for a second before he said, "President Achari, may I suggest that you speak with a very wise man, one who was of great assistance to me when my country was attacked."

"You know, Jim, I think it could be done. A fleet of small hybrids, energy efficient, and the drivers could come from the pool of people we are teaching to be self-sufficient."

"That would work, but the mechanics need some thought."

John leaned back in his chair, staring at the flames crackling over the logs. "Catherine," he said, "always lights the fire here in the study when she knows that I am stressed. It calms me, and helps me to think. My heart is breaking for India and her people, and we are poised on the edge of what could become a world-wide conflict. I feel like Kennedy. Never thought that would happen."

"Mumbai's a lot farther away than Cuba," Jim commented.

"And distance matters a lot less now than it did then. We really have become a global village."

John's cell phone rang, and he tossed it to Jim. "See who that is, will you, and tell them I'll call them back. I need to think. There must be something I can do."

"You can take this call," Jim said. "It's Aadil Achari."

While the two statesmen began their conversation, Jim slipped from the room. He quickly and quietly returned with Catherine and Carolyn, and the three of them took seats and shamelessly eavesdropped.

John had set his cell phone on the table beside Catherine's Sevres vase. The speaker was on, and John was standing staring out of the window, so immersed in what Aadil Achari was saying that he neither saw the gardens in front of him, nor registered the fact that he was not alone.

"I'm pleased that Anthony felt I was of some help to him when the terrorists," he said. "It was a terrible time for the British, as you can now fully appreciate, Prime Minister. Oh, yes, of course, Aadil, but only if you call me John. Anthony is turning into a fine leader. I'm proud of him."

"You are right, John. He has become, in fact, quite Churchillian. Or, perhaps, he simply resembles John Barton. I think that is how he would put it."

"Then he would be giving me too much credit," John said. "How are you coping, Aadil? How are your people?"

"They are stunned, John, and afraid, and grief stricken, and angry. I have a terrible decision to make."

"And, if I remember correctly, you adhere to Gandhi's principals of non-violence."

"I do, but they do not blind me to reality, John. I see this attack for what it is, and I am so furious that I am afraid of what I might do."

"Tell me. I need to understand this from your point of view."

Aadil Achari took a deep breath, and sighed, "I believe what Tariq Khan told me. This was not government authorized, John. It is more sinister than that, if that is possible."

"The Caliphate?" John asked.

"Or some similar Islamic group. Khan and Malik think either the I.S.I., or a splinter section of the military. It really doesn't matter. This is an effort to weaken us. We are a buffer between China and the rest of the world, and we keep that land in check. We shall watch as the western nations react to this attack. If we do not like what they do, then our relations with them will be weakened. If that happens, then China will seize the opportunity to flex its muscles, and India will be in jeopardy. We have learned to live with our Muslim neighbors, but we do not forget, for one instant, that many of them would like to see us all worship Islam."

"And that includes my new country, and the United States," John said. "I see what you are facing."

"Yes, John," Aadil Achari said, "but can you put yourself in my shoes?"

"May I try," John asked, "and may I begin with an example you will at first find repugnant."

"Now I am curious. After today, repugnance will not be easy. Please, speak to me."

"Nathuram Godse."

"Godse? The man who shot Gandhi Ji."

"Yes, Aadil. Was he Moslem?"

"Ah, John! You would not ask that question if you did not know the answer. No, Godse was Hindu. He believed that the Mahatma was growing too close to the Islamic communities, and that his faith was threatened by this."

"Yes, and he blamed Gandhi for the partition of India, and for all who died because of it. He felt that a Hindu, despite the faith's teachings, has a right to fight when his way of life is threatened."

"And you would hold this assassin up to me as an example, John? This cannot be why Anthony asked me to call you."

"No, Aadil. No. Godse's beliefs led him to commit a terrible act, as terrible as the launching of this missile by men who, despite the teachings of Islam, chose to turn to violence in what they feel is the righteous promulgation of the one true faith. Both are equally wrong, but does that mean that defending one's way of life is also evil?"

Aadil Achari thought for a long moment before he reluctantly said, "No."

"So, Aadil, we now know that you are courageous, because it takes courage to acknowledge that the peaceful way will not always work, no matter how much we wish it could be so. Neither, in this instance, will unspeakable violence carried out for nothing more than revenge."

"I know that, John, and I am ashamed of how much I want it."

"I don't think that you really do, Aadil, and I, too, believe Tariq Khan, but he must also face facts. It was possible for this to happen because his administration is corrupt, feckless, and weak. Weak, Aadil, and that is a perception India cannot afford. Lie down under this, and your land will be ravaged, the wolves and the jackals will eat away at your borders, while their weapons devastate your interior, and India will fall."

"What must I do," Aadil Achari asked.

"When I.S.I. trained Islamic militants attacked your hotels in Mumbai, killing your citizens and your nation's guests, you did nothing. When those same militants staked out one of the few Jewish synagogues in your nation of more than one billion people, then slaughtered the Rabbi and his family, you failed to respond. In light of today's events, Aadil, I must ask you, has this policy of non-violence helped your people?"

"May Ram forgive me," Aadil Achari said. "No, John, it has not."

"And if your people see that you do nothing now, they will feel victimized and weak, and they will become prey for the jackal and the wolf. If you launch an all out attack on Pakistan, you will involve the rest of the world, and millions, or even billions will die. You will have become part of the evil. But, evil, Aadil, is not afraid of good. It wishes only to destroy it. Evil is afraid only of strength greater than its own. When faced with this strength, it reveals itself as the coward it is, and it turns tail and runs. Your people deserve to see this. Your dead are crying for it."

"So I must retaliate?"

"Yes, Aadil, you must, in the proper manner. For India."

"Innocent beings will die if I do this, John. Children will die."

"They died today, Aadil, and your past actions were partly responsible."

"No one else on earth, John Barton, would have the courage to say this to me."

"But many of your people may be thinking it, Aadil."

There was silence, and the three people listening to the conversation held their breath.

"Barrington-Worley was right to have me call you," Aadil Achari said. "I assume that you have some targets in mind?"

"Two, Aadil. I would blow up the I.S.I. headquarters and everyone in it, and I would drop several bombs on the military installation at Abbottabad. Bin Laden lived there safely for so many years, and he was killed there. India's action will send a threefold message. First, the I.S.I. will be treated as an independent force. Secondly, the military will be treated as an independent force until it has proved otherwise and, thirdly, the radical Islamists will know they are in your sights and targeted by your nation."

"May I not warn them, John, so that the innocent may leave?"

"The innocent, Aadil, probably do not have the means to leave. Only the guilty will flee."

"And this must happen at once?"

"Yes, it must. Your people will sleep easier tonight because of it, and Pakistan, if it is true that the government did not authorize this attack, will not respond."

"It is true, John, I am sure of that."

"Then let us deal with the aftermath. When these reprisals are completed, I would suggest that you address your nation and request television and radio transmission into Pakistan. You should state clearly that the response by India was not directed at the elected government, or the people, of Pakistan. You should reiterate the fact that President Khan did not order the initial attack. Tell them that you do not apologize for defending your nation against independent actions taken by the I.S.I. and the Pakistani military. Remind the people of both lands that they once fought together to end British colonial rule, and that they were brothers and sister then. Tell them that they now need to work together as neighbors to bring the I.S.I and the military under the control of the elected leaders of Pakistan. Ask them to pray with you, no matter what their faith, for an end to these attacks and for peace. End by saying it is your fervent hope that there is no retaliation against this just reprisal. Tell them there has been enough death. Ask them, instead, to join you in a vigil. To watch the sun rise the next morning, and give thanks that they are there to witness such a miracle."

"And while I do this terrible thing, John Barton, will you pray for my soul?"

"Gladly, Aadil Achari, if you will also pray for mine."

chapter

EIGHT

"Madam President, there seems to be a consensus. We all strongly recommend that you make this trip."

Edwina Boulder looked around the Oval Office. Martine was perched on one of the sofas, long legs slanted to one side and neatly crossed at the ankles. Pershing Amhurst, who was serving the second year of his term as Chairman of the Joint Chiefs of Staff, stood ramrod straight in front of the French door to her right. Edwina realized that she had seldom seen the man sit down, and was forced to wonder if he had trained himself to sleep standing up. Minority Leader, Billy Hutzman, sat facing her, his elbows on his knees, watching intently for her reaction to his statement, and her Press Secretary, Hailey Miles, who had been with her for years, sat next to him, nodding her agreement.

"I don't want to," she said, as if this were enough to settle the matter once and for all. She picked up her pen and began leafing through the documents on her desk, ignoring them all, and hoping that they would take this as the dismissal it was meant to be. They did not.

"Ma'am," Hailey Miles said, clearing her throat nervously, "Prime Minister Barrington-Worley will be there, as will the French Premier, and Chancellor Engela Metz."

"The Germans are going? What an honor for India and Pakistan. Get the Veep. He needs something to do."

"The Vice President will be in Afghanistan," Martine said. "The trip's been scheduled for a while. He can't call it off. Even the Chinese are sending a delegation."

"Why all this fuss over a memorial service?" Edwina asked.

"Because, Ma'am," Pershing Amhurst said, "the governments of the two countries and their stricken people have, with a great deal of self-control and constraint, refrained from plunging this world into what could well have been a nuclear conflagration. They deserve our respect and our gratitude, along with our reassurance that those they mourn have not died in vain."

"Send flowers."

"Ma'am," Martine chimed in, "with your permission, may I be a little more specific about the agenda for this event?"

"Go ahead if you want, but it won't change my mind."

Martine leafed through the papers on her clipboard, found the one she wanted and said, "The first memorial service will be in Mumbai, at the site of the initial attack. The President and Prime Minister of Pakistan will attend, as will a large number of ordinary citizens from Pakistan who lost relatives and loved ones in the retaliatory strike. Two days later, there will be a similar ceremony at what was Pakistan's I.S.I HQ. A comparable number of India's bereaved will attend. The intervening day allows for a rest from travel, and provides the attending heads of state with a chance to meet with one another."

"It will be hot," Edwina Boulder said. "I hate the heat. I sweat, no matter what I do, and I will look like shit on all the video coverage. Send the Veep. He's mainline Philadelphia. Those people never sweat."

Martine sighed and leaned back against the sofa, admitting defeat. She glanced at Hutzman and Hailey, and they all looked at Pershing Amhurst, who stared straight ahead, refusing to meet their eyes.

Billie Hutzman got up and headed for the door. "I don't think we should take up any more of your valuable time, Madam President," he said as he opened it. "By the way, I don't think anyone's mentioned that John Barton will be there."

"Wait," Edwina said. "Shut that door and sit down. Why's Barton going? He isn't even a head of state until after the election."

Billie Hutzman told her all he knew about John Barton's role in averting the crisis, and then the President of the United States called the Executive Residence and told the staff to start packing.

John Barton stood by the stream, opposite the dead oak tree, Dillon at his side. It had become, for him, a place of comfort and contemplation, and he wished he had time to visit it more often. He had come there on the day India launched its retaliatory strike. He had sat on the bank, his arm around Dillon's massive shoulders, and he had stroked the dog, staring at the water and saying nothing as he imagined the carnage taking place on the other side of the world, carnage he had instituted. He would have to bear the burden for many years to come, and his heart ached for Aadil Achari, a man of peace who would be forced to do the same.

When he was sure that the attack must be over, John Barton had risen to his feet and become aware once more of the peace around him. Dillon sat gazing up at him, his brown eyes filled with concern.

"Well, boy," John told him as they turned and headed for the house, "I'm responsible for the loss of many lives, and I can only pray that I have saved millions more."

That had been the time of horror, and this was time to heal. John had worked closely with the leaders of both nations to plan these memorials. They had agreed with him that the presence of representatives from each country, on the other's soil, was vital. "It is hard," Aadil Achari said when it was decided, "to regard a person as an enemy once you have dried their tears."

John had been invited to attend, as a private citizen representing the Free States of America. He had tried to decline, not wanting to distract the press from the ceremonies that should be the focus of its attention, but he had not been allowed to do so, and he and Catherine were leaving that evening, along with Jim and Caroline.

"Time for a stroll before I finish packing," he told the dog, who barked his appreciation.

The security guards who followed him at a discreet distance each thought, without the other being aware of it, that they had never seen John Barton looking so utterly alone.

There had not been time to clear Mumbai's Ground Zero, that would take months, maybe years, but this was India, and the ravaged land was covered with flowers whose colors blazed in the sunshine. Everyone except the men from the west wore white, the Hindu color of mourning, and many tears were shed. Hindu and Moslem widows, fathers, mothers, brothers, sisters, and children stood hand in hand, or with arms around one another, giving and receiving comfort in equal measure, united by their grief.

It was a harrowing day.

John Barton stepped out onto the balcony of his hotel room early the next morning, and would not have been surprised if he had been told that he had entered paradise. The air was cool, and made cooler by the water that had been used to wash paths and water beds. The sky was clear and blue, and the greens in the lush hotel garden were so intense that they almost hurt the eye. There were flowers everywhere, their scent mixing with the spicy tang of Indian cooking to create an aroma that could not be duplicated anywhere else on earth. No voices could be heard, and the only man John could see was tending to some plants, his movements gentle and unhurried, in harmony with the land. The air was filled with birdsong, and flashes of brilliant color darted among the trees. John drew what felt like the first really deep breath he had taken for days. He lifted his head and silently thanked his Maker for the gift of such glory.

And his cell phone rang.

The screen read 'Private', which tweaked John's curiosity. "Herr Barton," a soft voice said when he answered, "This is Engela Metz."

"Good morning, Madam Chancellor. I have to admit that this is a surprise. I wish that I could greet you in German."

"This is not a problem, Herr Barton. I have been told that my English is very good, though, as you well know, no one in my position can be sure that a compliment is sincere. You will tell me at once if you do not understand me, ja?"

John assured Germany's Chancellor that he would do so, and she went on, "Herr Barton, might you have time to meet with me today?"

"Of course, Madam Chancellor. Where and when?"

"As soon as possible, I think," she said. "While others may still be sleeping, or dawdling over the beginning of the day. I am glad that I was correctly told that you are an early riser."

"Just tell me where," John said.

"Ah, Herr Barton, this is the difficulty. I would like this meeting to pass unnoticed by the press, or any of our fellow guests. I am unsure where to go to accomplish this."

"You are at the German consulate?" John asked.

"Ja, naturlich."

"Listen, then. I have an idea."

Fifteen minutes later, the Chancellor of Germany and the future president of the Free States of America were in a storeroom that opened off the hotel kitchen.

"I feel like a girl playing hide and seek," Engela said smiling broadly, "and I have not taken a taxi for years. I enjoyed that. Excuse me while I return to being myself." The Chancellor whipped off a long dark wig, dropped it to the floor, and ran her fingers through her hair as she turned to survey the small room. Cans and jars lined shelves. "Look at all this food. Do you know what we would have given for this in East Germany when I was a child?"

"It must have been hard, Chancellor."

"It was, John, and you will call me Engela, ja? When I was a teenager, I felt that I would never live to see my country reunited, but look at us now. Anything is possible. I have learned this, and so have you."

"Three impossible things before breakfast," John said.

"Alice," Engela announced. "It is a wonderful book. I read it often to my children, and now to their little ones."

"Sometimes," John said, "just believing hard enough in them can make them come true."

"Ja, and you are a fine example of this," she said, sitting on a rice sack opposite him. "It is hard for you now, this I know. Remember, John, Germany at the end of World War two. Hitler's Reich collapsed, and we were a broken people, without any hope or any future, and we were crippled by shame over what had been done in our name. We were a nation divided, and our economy was as dead as our insane Fuehrer. We received assistance from England, from the USA and from the allies who defeated the evil that was rampant in our land. We persevered, and our future is bright.

You must do the same. I am most interested in your plans for your new country."

"I am flattered to hear that, Engela. You have guided your land to an era of unprecedented prosperity. I should very much like to follow your example."

"Prosperity, ja. I often feel like one who secured a large lottery prize. All I ever get is begging letters, either literally or, what is the word, metaphorically?"

"I had not thought of that. Being the wealthiest country in the European Union has to have its drawbacks."

"It does, John, and the union itself causes many of them."

"Tell me."

The Chancellor of Germany curled her legs underneath her. John noticed that she was wearing American jeans, and that they flattered her neat figure. Engela Metz was tiny, a fact John had never realized from watching her on the news. Her close cropped blonde hair lay in crisp curls on a well-shaped skull, and large blue eyes gave her look of an elf surprised in some woodland glade. It was hard to believe that she was one of the most powerful women in the world until, that is, one remembered the brilliant and razor sharp mind that dwelt behind those glowing eyes.

"Let us," she said, "as it seems we so often must, go back before we go forward. You have time, ja?"

John nodded, and Engela went on, "Long before I had even thought of being in politics, although I found them fascinating from the time I could begin to understand, Europe's leaders wanted to make a union. They did not want a federation, like the United States, with one government presiding over the state's legislatures, a common foreign policy and a national military. They thought, rather, of an economic coalition, with free trade, open borders, and a single currency. So now we have the Euro, and we have chaos. The unions have grown so powerful that they are slowly strangling us. Our lips are already blue, and we shall soon be unable to continue to live."

"From what I've observed," John said, "it's as if they take turns striking."

"That is exactly what they do. One week the transport workers, another the pilots, the police, and then the sanitation workers. The list goes on and on, but it is the doctors who are the worst. We each have a national health program, which makes them public employees. It is unconscionable that they should strike, yet they do, and they allow their patients to die for lack of treatment."

"That should be enough to prevent them from practicing medicine again," John said.

"It should," Engela agreed, "but then where would we find the doctors to replace them. It is just one more cleft stick. Most of Europe's nations have been bankrupted by the entitlement programs they instituted. The people are insecure and desperate. The unions threaten, this leads to riots, then to strikes, and the whole cycle begins again. It cannot continue."

"How can it be stopped?" John asked.

The door opened, and a kitchen worker appeared. Smiling, but saying nothing, he set a brass tray of tea between them, slung a bag of rice over his shoulder and left.

"How kind these people are," Engela said. "I wonder what those little patties are. They smell good, and I am hungry. Shall I pour?"

"No," John said. "I'll do it. You go on talking."

"Well, John, to answer your question, I do not know how to stop it, not for the whole union. So I must think first of Germany. Every crisis ends with a phone call to me. 'We need your help and the help of Germany'.

"Can you go on supporting the rest of Europe?"

"Maybe, our economy is thriving, and only Ireland is even comparable, but do I want to? I am not helping them. I am just helping to perpetuate an untenable situation. Ah, my high school English teacher would be proud of me for that sentence."

They laughed together, and Engela picked up one of the samosas and ate it in two bites.

"That is so good," she said. "Do you know what it is?"

"I think it is filled with potatoes and peas," John told her.

"That sounds very boring. It must be the spices that make it taste so wonderful. So, John Barton, we have reached the point where I must tell you why I wanted to meet with you. Are you ready?"

"I think so," John said. "Although I am beginning to realize that you are a most unpredictable Chancellor."

"Not a bit like my famous iron predecessor? That is good. Listen, John, I wish to break my country away from this union. I wish to make a new currency, in which Germany will deal, and I should like to create this innovation with you, and the Free States of America."

"John?" the Chancellor asked several seconds later, "are you all right? Is this such a terrible idea?"

"Only if a dream coming true is a bad thing," John said. "If there were room in here, I would be dancing. Why would you want to do this? My tiny nation may fail before it has properly drawn breath."

"No, John, it will not. I have spoken at length with my three top advisors. They tell me that it is only a matter of time before many other states join your confederation. You will eventually replace the USA, hard as it may be to believe right now."

"What makes you so sure, Engela?"

"You have had the courage to begin in the right way, John. Your new constitution will limit the Socialists, and the organizations they spawn and stretch, like tentacles, across the land. With us behind you, you will become an economic powerhouse, and the next great superpower. It is as simple as that."

"So the richest country in Europe wants to be the partner of a small, and far from wealthy, state, and launch a globally accepted currency?"

"Yes, and yes again, John. We want you to succeed. This marriage allows us to divorce ourselves from Europe, and this must be done. I am told that you plan on running your country as if it were a corporation. Think of us as your venture capitalists."

"I will discuss this with my advisors," John told her, "and I think they will be as excited at the prospect as I am. So, Madam Chancellor" he went on, raising his teacup, "let us drink to our engagement.

"Catherine?"

"Yes."

"It's Jim."

"I know. How are you on this lovely morning?"

"I'm fine, Catherine. Is Caroline with you?"

"No, Jim, she's not."

"I don't understand it. She was gone when I woke up. No note, nothing, and she's not answering her cell. Where can she be?"

"Oh, I'm pretty sure I know, Jim, and if you think for a moment, you will, too."

Catherine ended the call, and Jim Eliades stared at his cell phone as if it might furnish the answer he wanted. What if she had been kidnapped? He realized that he was annoyed at Catherine for taking this so lightly. It wasn't like her to exhibit such a lack of concern, and how could she possibly know where Caroline was? She could be anywhere in this huge, disaster torn city.

Disaster?

Jim Eliades left the hotel and headed straight for the American Consulate.

He found her in the third of the buildings on the list the consular official had given him. The room was clean, but bare except for rows of small beds. It was full of children with bandaged limbs and heads, hard casts, and multiple bruises. Crutches were propped against the wall, and Caroline sat on one of the beds, holding its occupant's hand. A baby was nestled in the crook of the other arm, and children were clustered around her, leaning on her knees, jostling one another to get close to her, chattering like starlings, and laughing.

It was the laughter that amazed Jim the most as he watched from the doorway. Had it been heard much in this room before his Caroline arrived? He somehow doubted it.

Caroline saw him, and waved him over. He went to her, leaned over the small bodies and kissed the top of her head.

"I was worried," he said.

"Were you, my darling?" Caroline asked, turning to look up at him. "I am so sorry."

"Not really worried. More frantic, I think."

"I thought you would know," she said, "that I have work to do here."

"I should have. Catherine did. Are these children all orphans?"

"Yes. Some of them were before this happened. They were probably living on the streets. Others lost their parents in the attack. It must be hardest for them."

"They all look happy enough now."

"That's because something is going on, and they are children, easily distracted. Bedtime is the hardest when you are little and you feel lost and alone."

"Did you feel that way?" Jim asked, walking around the bed so that he could see her face. The children watched him, quiet now and brown eyes huge as they tried to gauge whether this large person had come to spoil their fun. A tiny boy began to scale Jim's leg, his own limbs locked around it as if it were a piece of playground equipment. Jim plucked him off, lifted and turned him, and seated him on his shoulder. The child clutched, rather painfully, at his hair.

"You're probably the tallest person he's ever seen," Caroline commented. "Hence the urge to climb you."

"I feel a bit like Everest right now," Jim told her. "It's not a bad feeling. Did you?"

"Feel that way? Yes, when I was very small, and my father was so grief stricken over my mother's death that he could not bear to look at me. There were nannies, and they were kind, but it wasn't the same."

"You'll be back here at bedtime, won't you?" Jim asked.

"Yes, I'll be here and at the other three shelters."

"And you aren't coming back with us."

"No, my love. I'm needed here."

"Yes," he said. "I can see that you are."

She smiled up at him, and the baby began to cry.

Catherine and John enjoyed a wonderful lunch at their hotel, reveling in the taste of the spicy food, and then they separated. John joined President Tariq Khan and Prime Minister Kareem Malik, and the three of them took a short flight to Lahore, the second largest city in Pakistan, and the one often referred to as the heart of the nation. Catherine and Aadil Achari flew to India's Amritsar.

Each in an air conditioned limousine, the Bartons were given tours of the respective cities. Each of them used their cell phones to capture images of ancient and glorious temples and mosques, impossibly crowded streets, the roadside vendors of everything from vegetables to carved furniture, and soaring modern architecture sitting comfortably side by side with edifices many centuries older than their own country. Neither of them could wait to share the pictures with the other.

As sunset approached, each of them was driven the short distance to the Wagah Border Crossing. There, from specially designated sections of the stands, they joined the thousands who gather daily to watch the evening ceremonies.

The bricks from which the Pakistani gatehouse was constructed were the soft pink of a faded rose, and they glowed as the sun dropped lower. Wrought metal gates spanned the archway. They were painted the dark green of the nation's flag, with the white crescent moon and star standing out in stark contrast. Pakistani Rangers guarded the border. Each of them stood at least six foot four, and the cockaded turbans they wore made them appear at least a foot taller than that. Their uniforms were black, accented with scarlet bordered belts, the tails of their turbans flowed stiffly starched down their backs, bobbing as they moved, and an array of medal ribbons decorated each broad chest. Scarlet bands wrapped their turbans, and their black cockades sprang from golden bases. They were, by any standards, an impressive group of men.

The Indian Border Guards wore khaki, with belts of black and red and gold. Scarlet and gold cockade towered over pugarees of the same colors. They looked like the warriors they were. The gates they guarded were curved and more ornate. From Pakistan, they were simply white. From the other side, they were emblazoned with the red and green of the Indian flag, and gold lettering stood out against the red.

The performance that ensued was a marvelous display of bellowed orders that echoed in the still air, precision marching, high stepping that would have done an acrobat justice, and men strutting like peacocks. They closed and reopened both sets of gates; ventured across the white painted line that bisected the no man's land in between them, indicating the border; glaring fiercely at one another as they mimicked invasion. Then they retreated and rejoined, each squad on its own land. They vied to yell the loudest, kick the highest, and stare with the greatest aggressiveness, and they did it all with an underlying humor and a sense of companionship that made the display memorable.

As the sun set, trumpets sounded and the flags of each land were simultaneously lowered, remaining side by side for an instant before they were removed, ceremoniously folded, and marched, with all due respect, from the parade ground. On either side of the border, patriots cheered them to their rest.

When it was over, buses pulled up at each set of gates, their passengers disembarked, crossed the border, and climbed aboard the waiting buses on the other side. The two vehicles turned and resumed their journeys, one headed back to Amritsar, and the other toward Lahore.

Lights were twinkling in the twilight, and spotlights were suddenly trained on the white line that divided what had, for centuries, been one nation. John Barton stepped into their glare, and stood with his feet straddling the line. Catherine joined him there. Tariq Kahn and Raheem Malik appeared, the Rangers in close formation behind them, and the Border Guard parted to allow President Achari to walk between them, then rejoined, standing at attention behind him.

The crowds had been preparing to leave, but the lights and the movement caught their attention, and most of them returned to their seats. Members of the media appeared on either side of the white line, focusing cameras on the spotlighted dignitaries.

Microphones were placed, and Aadil Achari stepped forward. "I am a child of India," he said, "and I stand on my own land."

"And I on mine," Tariq Khan announced.

"I cherish the earth of Pakistan," said Raheem Malik.

"Between us stands a man from another continent," Achari continued. "Symbolically, he has one foot in each of our lands, for, more than any other man alive, he has the right to stand there."

"When a renegade section of Pakistan's armed forces launched an attack on India," Tariq Kahn said, "we stood on the brink of a terrible war."

"Thousands of lives were lost," Malik added, "and millions more were in peril."

"India had the right to revenge its dead," Achari said.

"And Pakistan stood ready to defend its land," Malik solemnly stated.

"Such conflicts can far too easily escalate," Tariq Khan said, "and we faced the possibility of a nuclear winter falling on this region of warmth and light."

"As Ghandi and Jinnah stood on the eve of partition, knowing that they risked lighting the fuse of a powder keg that would destroy all they loved and had fought for," Achari said.

"So we three men, two presidents and a prime minister, stood in awe of the power we held in those hours," Tariq Khan finished for him.

"We could not afford one false step," Malik said. "We could not afford emotion, yet each nation's pride had to be satisfied. There seemed to be no way to accomplish this."

"Yet this man found one," Achari said, indicating John.

"His wise council guided us," Tariq Khan said, "when we were most in need of guidance."

"And the solution he proposed punished the guilty, and was the most merciful for the innocent," Malik stated.

"Lives were lost," Achari sadly said, "and that is hard to bear, hard for the people of both our nations, but countless lives were saved because of John Barton."

"We have, therefore, jointly authorized the creation of a new and unique order," Malik said.

"The Order of Unity will be bestowed only with the consent of those three individuals who hold the offices we are now privileged to enjoy," Achari said.

"It will represent both Pakistan and India," Tariq Khan explained, "and those so honored will have demonstrated service that promotes unity, friendship, and mutual honor and respect amongst both our peoples."

"The first member of this order will be John Barton," Achari said, "and the medal will be presented by Daksha Agrawal and Hussein Buledi, each of whom lost their families in the attacks. They will represent the unity John Barton has done so much to foster."

Two children stepped into the limelight. The tiny girl who came from the Indian side wore a red and gold sari, and flowers were tucked into the thick braid of hair that hung down her back. She was too shy to look at anyone but the boy who walked toward her through the other gate, and her dark eyes were huge and filled with admiration and trust when she looked up at him. He joined her and took her hand. The boy carried himself proudly. He wore the traditional long jacket and tight scrunched trousers known as the Sherwari, and a Jinnah cap, named after the founder of Pakistan, was on his head.

A Ranger and a Border Guard appeared behind the children, jointly bearing a velvet cushion on which a medal reposed. The four of them approached John and Catherine, and the soldiers snapped to attention. They then bent at the waist, holding the cushion out to the children. They solemnly grasped the ribbon on which the medal hung and turned to John. He bent low, and the ribbon was placed around his neck. When he straightened, the gold bright against his chest, trumpets sounded and the children bowed. Two presidents and a prime minister did the same, and the crowd followed suit.

After that, the cheering began. It grew louder when Catherine picked up the little girl and kissed her. John lifted Hussein and held him high, looking up at him and laughing.

Flashbulbs made the spotlights look dim by comparison.

"Turn it off," Edwina Boulder commanded. "That damned man has his fingers in every pie. Can't even turn on the news in the morning without hearing Barton, Barton, Barton. I'm sick of the sound of his name.

Martine Rivers took the remote and turned off the TV. "You have a couple of free hours, Madam President," she said. "What would you like to do with them?"

There was a reception at the American Consulate that evening, a final opportunity to mix and mingle before the politicians returned to their own capitals. The consulate was in the Bandra Kurla Complex, which was on the edge of the blast area. Some damage could be seen to the exterior, but the building was relatively new, and the construction was strong, so business continued as usual inside.

The room was full when John, Catherine, and Jim arrived. There was a low hum of conversation, but the mood felt subdued and filled with respect. Engela Metz, wearing a simple sapphire blue sheath that matched her eyes, was chatting with a group of professors from the University of Mumbai. The French Premier towered over the Chinese delegation, and had bent like a bow so that he could hear what the tiny interpreter, who looked as if she had been carved from tawny ivory, was saying. Anthony Barrington-Worley waved at them from across the room, raising his glass in a silent toast. Secret Service agents, almost comically vigilant, ringed the room. If they were making any attempt at blending in, they were failing miserably.

"So the President plans on being fashionably late," Catherine murmured.

"No point in arriving until a crowd has gathered to applaud the entrance," Jim muttered in her ear. "That's politics 101."

Catherine was laughing when the Marine guards on either side of the door snapped audibly to attention, and a disembodied voice announced, "Ladies and gentlemen, the President of the United States."

Edwina Boulder, who was wearing stark black, strode unescorted into the room, followed by a retinue of staff members that included Martine Rivers. Only a flick of the president's eyes betrayed, as she passed John, the fact that she had registered his presence. She was greeted by the Consul General, photographs were taken, and she became the immediate focal point of the room, with supposedly sophisticated guests jockeying, as subtly as they could, for places that would guarantee them her notice.

"Let's go and get a drink," John said. "It's getting crowded at this end of the room."

A noted Pakistani economist recognized John and buttonholed him and Catherine, eager to discuss John's plans for the Free States. Jim had just taken his first sip of his Scotch and soda when a voice from behind him said, "It's good to see you and, believe it or not, I truly mean that."

"Hello, Martine," he said without turning. "How's life in the White House?"

"Jim, I know you must be very angry with me, but ... "

He turned to face her then, and saw that she was as glorious as ever in a dress of dull bronze, its skirt slit high to reveal those fabulous legs. "Angry?" he repeated. "No, on the contrary, Martine, I owe you a deep debt of gratitude."

"Gratitude?" she asked, looking puzzled and, for once, unsure of herself.

"Yes. You see, when you have learned to spot a fake, painful as the experience may be, it is easier to know the real thing when you are fortunate enough to come across it."

"I deserve that," Martine said, her eyes shining with tears. "So you are in love. Is she here?"

"No, she is tucking her children into bed."

"She has children?"

"Yes, hundreds of them, maybe thousands, and she is the only mother each of them has."

"A Mother's Love," Martine gasped. "I've heard about her. Isn't she fabulously rich?"

"She is fabulously rich in loving kindness," Jim said. "And she bestows it on everyone around her. As for the money, she spends more time giving that away than most people spend acquiring it. I think the president is trying to get your attention."

"Oh! Yes, she is. Thanks," Martine said, moving a few steps away from him, then turning back. "And Jim ... "

"Yes, Martine."

"One part of it was real, though I didn't know it for a while."

"Really? And which part was that?"

"I did love you, and I still do."

Jim watched as Martine crossed the room, and wondered why he felt absolutely nothing.

Martine bent down so that she could hear Edwina speak softly into her ear, her face averted from those around her.

"Me?" she protested softly. "Must I? Can't someone else do it?"

One look at the president's face told her that they could not, and it took all the courage she had to walk up to them.

John reached for Catherine's hand, and the two of them looked at the woman who had betrayed their kindness and lied about an affair with John, all in an effort to sabotage his presidential campaign. They watched her approach them, and they said nothing. They didn't have to. It was all written on their faces, and Martine could feel their contempt. And their pity, which was far harder to bear. She had to swallow and wet her lips before she managed to say, "President Boulder would be happy if you could spend a few minutes with her."

"I wonder if the choice of a messenger was meant more to hurt us or you," John said.

"Her," Catherine said. "The poor child is shaking."

"Please go away," John said, drawing Catherine closer to his side. "We shall, of course, do as the president asks."

Martine glanced around before she walked, on legs that wobbled just a little, in what she fervently hoped was the direction of the ladies' room.

"That was unspeakably cruel of Edwina", Catherine said.

"Yes," John agreed. "It can't be very comfortable working for the most powerful woman in the world, particularly when she misuses that power."

He took Catherine's elbow, and they crossed the room toward Edwina, who was speaking with Anthony Barrington-Worley.

"Mr. Prime Minister," she said, "how nice to see John Barton's champion in the flesh. Charles Dudley Warner should be proud of himself right now."

"Ah, the man who said that politics makes strange bed-fellows," Barrington-Worley said. "Yes, ma'am, I had heard rumors that this is so."

He glanced pointedly at Martine, who was disappearing through an archway. Edwina froze, staring at him with a loathing most adults reserve for maggots. Only the Barton's arrival jerked her back to the business at hand. "Ah," she said. "Benedict Arnold, I believe."

"No, Madam President, just John Barton. May I present my wife, Catherine?"

Edwina glanced at Catherine, nodding briefly before she turned her attention back to John. "You have such a talent, Mr. Barton, for capturing the headlines. It is nice to see that they have been, recently at least, favorable."

"Like all politicians, ma'am," John countered, "I can only hope that this continues, whilst knowing that it will not."

"The hero of the hour, Mr. Barton. I feel quite privileged. And all this without even currently holding office. It's quite miraculous, and how are the Free States, or should that be state? Prospering I hope."

"We expect that we shall do so in time, ma'am. For the present, we are more concerned with getting ourselves organized."

"Another presidential campaign, Governor Barton. You must be quite tired of them by now. Shall you see this one through to the bitter end?"

The group around the president sensed the hostility in the exchange and grew quiet, glancing from Edwina to John, eager to hear what came next. Barrington-Worley grimaced in disgust, nodded to John and Catherine, and drifted away.

"Indeed I shall, ma'am," John said, "although I hope the end will not be bitter. There is a sweetness to a new beginning, and I should like to preserve that."

"I hope that you are able to do so, Governor, but beginnings can be costly, as much for a nation as they are for a small business."

John smiled down at her. "You are, of course, correct, Madam President, but some things are worth doing, no matter what the cost. Will you excuse us? We must not monopolize your time."

Edwina nodded, and John and Catherine walked away.

"You are shaking," John said. "In any other woman, I would think it was nerves, but you, you are laughing."

Catherine nodded, her eyes dancing. "Edwina," she said, "does not like losing, not even in a battle of wits. The look on her face was priceless. I thought she was going to spit at you like an angry cat." Then she gave up trying to conceal her enjoyment and laughed out loud.

Edwina Boulder turned instinctively toward the sound, and forgot, in mid-sentence, exactly what she had been saying to the ambassador from Sri Lanka.

chapter

NINE

For the next few weeks, John and Catherine criss-crossed the Free State of Georgia. It was somewhat less exhausting than trying to set foot in forty-nine more. They found themselves in areas even they had never visited before. They ate barbecue until the aroma of smoke clung to their hair and clothes, and they learned not to ask exactly what animal had been cooked for hours on a slow grill. Possum and squirrel taste a lot like beef, pork, or chicken when they are smothered in enough sweet and spicy sauce and served with some raw onions and a pickle or two.

On the up side, they met hundreds of the citizens of the Free States, listening to their opinions, addressing their concerns, and bolstering spirits that were already high. The Bartons even spent occasional nights at The Preserve, eat-ing a quiet dinner or picnicking with the kids and their families, then sleeping with Dillon cuddled between them, glad to be, at last, in their own bed.

The work on the stables was progressing well, Mike was responding to Mellie's excellent and loving care, and it looked as if they'd be able to move out of the apartment and into their new home in a month or, given the reliability of the average contractor, two at the most.

On the domestic front, the Barton's had no complaints.

On the political front, things were rather unnervingly calm. The media were covering the election process without any particular signs of bias, simply reporting on where the candidates were and what they had to say, without editorializing or indulging in ridicule or sarcasm.

It was almost too good to be true.

"Why would the Democratic Alliance hold its convention in Savannah?" Harris Gordon asked. "Been botherin' me ever since they announced it. Seems like the last place in the state, I mean the country ... haven't got used to it yet ... that lot would be sure of a warm welcome."

"Less of 'em to turn up?" Dallas Dee theorized. "Easier for those dinosaurs Knolls and Morse to push their boy's nomination through."

John's office at campaign headquarters grew quiet as everyone digested this. It was late, going on for two in the morning, and the rented store was finally quiet. Jim Eliades got up and made a circuit with the bourbon bottle, topping off everyone's glass. Tillie Gordon placed a hand over hers, and Jim gently nudged it aside. "Come on, Tillie. Been a hell of a day. Treat yourself."

Tillie smiled at him and moved her hand, and he let a mere splash of the liquor fall into her glass before he said, "Don't think it's that. The delegates will turn up anyway, and the rest of the political junkies will travel miles for a good convention, particularly one like this where they might even have some influence. No, it's more a matter of nasty, harsh political realities."

"Plenty of those to choose from," Dallas Dee grumbled. "Got one in particular in mind?"

"Yes," Jim said, "though you won't like it much."

"Don't like nothing much. Fire away."

"The young hopefuls," Jim said, reseating himself and raising an eyebrow at John, who was behind his desk, leaning back in his chair. When he received a grin and a nod, Jim heaved a sigh of relief, lifted his feet and lodged them on a corner of the desk. "God that feels good," he said. "Must've been on them since six this morning. Bet you could name a couple of them on the other side."

Without waiting for an answer, Jim went on, "But you don't see a lot of them clamoring for attention, do you?"

Dallas shook her head and yawned.

"No need to stay awake for this," Jim said. "We'll fill you in in the morning." Dallas glared at him. "It's pretty obvious that the liberals don't stand much hope this time around. Now, those young hopefuls, they want to some kind of a chance their first time out of the starting gate. If they don't get it, they're done. No matter how good they are, they're gonna be a Hubert Humphrey. Always a runner up."

"Can't argue with that," Tillie said.

"So what we're looking at here," Jim said, "is a young and inexperienced candidate who's the best of the bunch that volunteered for the suicide mission. The rest of them, the ones who might have stood some chance of winning, have backed off. They'll bide their time, and we'll hear from them loud and clear in four years, you mark my words."

"So this is a test run?" Tillie asked.

"In a way it's that for all of us," Jim told her. "No one can be positive how this new system will work, and it'll probably have to adapt itself a few times along the way."

"Least there won't be no socialists to hornswoggle us," Dallas commented.

"No, but there must be a healthy opposition," John said. "This *will* remain a democracy. We need to mold our policy on the environment, education, and health care, and we need to see all sides of the issues. There's taxes, and foreign policy, and areas we probably haven't even thought of yet. We have to deal with all of them. I hope this young man's more than a sacrificial lamb. We need good, cool heads at the table."

"No argument there, boss," Jim said. "But he's gonna stick his feet in the water, and the others are all gonna watch his face and gauge the temperature."

"Still doesn't explain Savannah," Harris Gordon commented.

"It's his home town," John said.

"Whose?"

"Jerome Green, the Democratic Alliance candidate for president. That's whose," Jim said. "Jeez, Harris, don't you listen to the news?"

"Aint had time. Been too busy campaigning for our side. Seen him on TV. Kid looks about sixteen."

"He's forty-four, Harris," Tillie told him. "Hasn't held any office other than the city council. They're pushing his 'fresh approach'."

"No big contributors to answer to?" Dallas asked. "No ties in government? No one who can call in favors? Didn't they try that once before?"

"Yeah," Jim said, "and they won."

"You're confusing me, Jim."

Everyone looked at John, and Jim asked, "How so, boss?"

"One minute they're running a lame duck, with no hope of success, and the next you remind us that an outsider can jog away with the race. Which is it?"

"Both," Jim said. "Or neither. This is an election. Anything can happen."

"Well, thanks for that," Dallas growled. "Guess we'll all sleep well tonight."

Two weeks later, the Democratic Alliance gathered in Savannah's International Trade and Convention Center, a mammoth and gleaming, white and many windowed building on the banks of the river and, after a week of meetings and parties, in about equal proportions, duly nominated Jerome Green as its candidate for president.

Green beamed as he stood center stage, one arm around his blonde wife, who was several inches taller than he was, and the other around his fourteen year old son's shoulders.

Green didn't have to reach up much to accomplish the latter. He was a lifelong democrat, the son of a union member and supporter, and he had served on Savannah's democratic committee for over ten years before anyone had noticed him and suggested that he be allowed to run for a vacant position on the city council. Devotion has its rewards, and the ward was mostly composed of mid-priced housing developments. Green won the election, and celebrated with a glass of non-diet soda. It was three months before he spoke at one of the council meetings. At that point, he addressed the budget, in minute detail. Jerome Green was, by profession, an accountant.

His running mate turned out to be a serious African American woman, a couple of years his senior. She had a successful husband, and she had devoted the years after her children had grown to working tirelessly as the unpaid president of an association that aided battered women and their children. Karen Andrews was far from uneducated, definitely well meaning, and about as interesting as a loaf of sliced bread.

Three weeks later, the National Modern Party members convened at the equally glossy and glassy Georgia International Convention Center, in Atlanta. On the final Saturday night, the huge hall was packed solid. There wasn't much doubt about the outcome. A couple of 'favorite sons' would receive token nominations from counties they had served in the former statehouse, and then it would be John Barton's turn. He and Catherine stood in the wings, the noise of the crowd washing over them, and quietly held hands.

Catherine could feel her husband's tension, and see it in the set of his shoulders and the tightness of his jaw. "Moses," she whispered.

"Moses, sweetheart?"

"Yes, John. He must have questioned himself, had second thoughts. Leading the Israelites out of slavery and across the desert can't have been an easy task."

"Don't suppose it was."

"And that's what you're doing, isn't it?"

"Me?"

"Yes, my John, you are leading our citizens to a new and better life, in a new and better land. You are our Moses."

"Moses! Good grief! Moses! That's it! God bless you, Catherine. Back in a moment."

John dashed away, heading for Jim Eliades. Catherine watched them as John hurriedly spoke; Jim looked puzzled for a second or two, then smiled, nodded, turned and hurried away.

"John," she asked when he returned to her side, "what's going on?"

"Something you set in motion," he said, squeezing her hand. "You'll see in a moment. Look, its nomination time."

Since John and Harris had no opposition from within the party, the usual nomination acceptance speeches had been removed from the program. Instead, a young and skinny black man, glancing nervously about him, walked into the spotlights and headed toward the mike. When he reached it, he cleared his throat and said, "Good evening."

He spoke so loudly that the scream of the electronic feedback was painful. "Sorry, he said. "Won't do that again.

My name is Randall Cummin, and I'm proud to be a citizen of the Free States of America. I guess I must have been born here, because I was abandoned, when I was just a few hours old, in a park in this city, in a trash can. I must have cried, because some kids found me and called the police. I don't know who those kids were, but I pray for them every day. I spent the next eighteen odd years in an orphanage, and I am old enough to vote.

"Now I'm willin' to bet that I'm the strangest speaker at one of these events any one of you has ever seen. I wasn't invited. I was just someone who helped out around campaign headquarters, and I asked to be here. I wanted it so much that I asked over and over again, every single day, until they gave in and told me I could be a delegate. Didn't expect top billing, but I can't tell you it's a bad feeling.

"I guess I'm like all of you. I got wants. I want to go to college. I want to make a difference, to the terrified young woman who threw me away, and to all those like her; to the people my age I've watched become addicted to drugs, and to all those who will follow them; and to all those who feel hopeless, helpless and alone. I've walked in their shoes.

"One day, I want to meet a girl and fall in love. I want to marry her, on a sunny morning I'll never forget, and I want to have kids. My family. I want to be able to take care of them. They should never be hungry, or afraid, they should never be like me.

"I have never had a home."

The entire auditorium was silent, and this seemed to worry Randall. "Look," he said, "this ain't no speech someone wrote for me. This is me, tellin' you what I feel. That's what they said I should do. Don't want to bore you, so please just listen for a coupl'a minutes longer.

"Like I said, I ain't never had a home, but I have one today. A whole nation is my home, and its people are my family, because I was there, I was part of making this country happen. I am no longer alone. I am one of you.

"An' we gotta chance, each one of us. We gotta chance to build a new land where all our wants will be taken into account. Gonna take a lot of hard work, 'n it won't be paradise, 'cause that ain't possible here on this earth. But it can be as good as it gets if we keep on heading in the right direction. Now we got a man, right back there, who's gonna see that we do just that. Don't think there's much else needs to be said.

"So here we are, makin' history. You 'n me. Don'tchya think it's time we got on with it?"

The crowd roared, and Randall reached out his arms. Making no effort to hide the tears that streamed down his cheeks, he said, "Let's do it. Let's do it together. My fellow delegates, it's my great honor and privilege to move that this august body nominate John Barton as the National Modern Party's candidate for the presidency of the Free States of America. All those in favor say 'Aye'."

It was over five minutes before the negligible 'Nay' vote could even be taken.

The crowd could not be quieted. Signs and banners were waved, hands clapped, feet stomped, and thousands of voices screamed for the man they had all come to see. Instead, Harris Gordon walked to the microphone. The lights flickered, and Jerusalem began to play. The final "Til we have built Jerusalem on this our green and pleasant land' almost lifted the rafters that rose high above the room.

No one minded giving their vocal chords a break after that. Harris did not waste the opportunity to be heard. "Ladies and gentlemen," he said. "Fellow members of the National Modern Party, fellow Free Staters, I want to thank you all for your devotion to this new land of ours, for your courage, and for your strength. It is now my privilege to call upon the Reverend Paul Donaldson, of St. Mark's church, who will invoke God's blessing upon these proceedings."

Harris stepped back and to the side, and his place was taken by the minister, who quietly said, "Let us pray."

As one, delegates rose to their feet and bowed their heads.

"Almighty God," Donaldson began, "creator of the universe, who reigns over all that it contains, be with us now. Bless this, our new country, those who live within its borders, and those who will lead it to a bright future, always keeping You as the burning light that guides them. Let the gift of your peace pervade our souls, ease our minds, and remain with us now and forever. We ask this in the name of your son, Jesus Christ our Lord. Amen."

The crowd echoed his final word, and he left the stage. Harris returned to the mike. "Don't bother to sit."

The lights dimmed, and the giant screens that ringed the auditorium lit up. Images of John holding Mike Newton after he had been shot, John with Queen Elizabeth, John with Prime Minister Barrington-Worley, John with the leaders of Pakistan and India, and John playing with Dillon and his grandchildren towered over the audience. Good luck messages from the Pope, the Archbishop of Canterbury and the Prime Minister of Israel played, and Jerusalem could once more be softly heard in the background.

Harris Gordon filled his mighty lungs and bellowed into the mike, "Ladies and Gentlemen, please welcome the next and first president of the Free States of America and his First Lady, John and Catherine Barton."

Hand in hand, John and Catherine walked across the stage. The barrage of sound that greeted them was almost palpable and, before it died down, they had plenty of time to reach the podium, wave, smile, find their family in their box and blow kisses to them and to the crowd in general.

John finally raised their clasped hands in a salute and said, "Thank you, Free Staters. Thank you for all that you are, and all that you do." He lowered their arms and took a step back, ceding precedence to the lady at his side. "This," he said, "as you all know, is my wondrous wife, Catherine, who never ceases to amaze me, even after all these years. She has no idea what a miracle she is. My Catherine reads my mind, knows when I am troubled and, without being aware that she is doing it, provides the solutions to my problems."

Catherine raised her eyebrows, and John said, "I can see that she is puzzled, and you may feel the same. Excuse me for one moment, and I will explain."

John escorted Catherine to a chair that had been placed for her, seated her, kissed her, and returned to the mike.

"Now," he said, "it is an awesome step that we have taken together. We have created a new country, and we must now decide how it will be governed. I have labored for hour upon hour over this. We know what we want to do, but what must be decided is the principles under which we shall accomplish this. What will be the foundation of the constitution that will guide us and mandate our progress into the future? Creating such a document is a task to be approached with reverence, with respect, and with a degree of terror. I have felt that terror. What we do now will influence the lives of many generations, and we must do it with great care."

John lowered his head and thought for a few seconds before he said, "We are about to elect a new government, and you have, today, accorded me the privilege and honor of possibly serving as its chief."

There were more cheers, and John waited for them to subside before he continued, "Quite naturally, the subject of our constitution has been uppermost on my mind this week. When we came here this evening, Catherine and I stood backstage, listening to what was going on. I still had no precise idea what I would say to you on the subject, should I be chosen to stand before you tonight. Catherine gave me the answer."

John turned and smiled at his wife, who blew him a kiss. Many members of the audience followed her example, and there was another hiatus before silence was restored.

"My wife," John said, "who must love me more than I deserve, saw that I was troubled and compared the task I am facing with the one Moses undertook when he led the Israelites out of slavery and across the deserts of Egypt, forging them into one people, one nation, as they traveled. One nation under one God.

"That was the answer. My gift from Catherine Barton. My gift and yours. Many of you are very familiar with the tenets upon which our constitution will be founded, but

I would ask you to read them with me once again." John turned his back to the audience and, on the giant screen they jointly faced, ten lines of text appeared. John turned to the microphone and slowly recited:

"Thou shalt have no other gods before me.

Thou shalt not make unto thee any graven images.

Thou shalt not take the name of the Lord thy God in vain.

Remember the Sabbath day, to keep it holy.

Honor thy father and thy mother.

Thou shalt not kill.

Thou shalt not commit adultery.

Thou shalt not steal.

Thou shalt not bear false witness against thy neighbor.

Thou shalt not covet.

"And there you have it, my fellow citizens, ten short sentences that tell us all the best way to live. Yet, when you look at these instructions, it is possible to see them another way. They could be summed up in the words, 'Thou shalt not steal'. Why? Because each of them involves taking something away from another human being, or from our God. The respect that is their due from Him, from the Sabbath, and from our parents. A life, a mate, property, the right to hear the truth, and the right to acquire land or objects without exciting envy and the reprisals it may engender. We may not lessen the lives of those around us in even the minutest manner. We must foster the general good in order to enjoy personal wellbeing.

"It took Catherine to show me how simple it was. The Free States of America will be dedicated to the Lord our God and, through Him and with Him, we shall set the world's standards for justice, equality of government, prosperity, and freedom. We will not forget where we come from, or where we are going.

Soon, you will be asked to vote on the new constitution and, at the same time, elect the first president of our country. You may vote for one, and not for the other, as you see fit. If you vote for me, you will be placing your future in my hands. In return, I will commit myself to ensuring that every citizen has the opportunity to excel. Whatever their color, religion or lifestyle, this government will assist them toward their goals. It will not be in place to hold some of you back, while others are pushed forward. It will respect the right to private property, and encourage success and the acquisition of wealth. It will, concomitantly, restrain its own role in your lives and its taxing power. This is true conservatism.

"I thank my wife for inspiring me, I thank you for your confidence in me, and I thank the God I will hold before me as we take this journey together. May He bless you and our nation."

The room exploded into cheers and applause. Catherine all but ran to John, and was enfolded in his arms for a moment. Their children and grandchildren joined them, as did a crowd of campaign workers, party dignitaries, and well-wishers. Harris Gordon and Tillie came to stand beside them, and balloons and confetti drifted down.

"It just doesn't feel right," David Canton said.

"Would that be the oversized cinnamon bun on which you are currently gorging, or your equally generous gut?" Billy Hutzman asked.

"Neither, though it rhymes nicely, Mr. Speaker. It's my butt."

"And that's not a subject I want discussed in my office," Martine Rivers snapped.

"Too bad," Canton retorted. "Despite your elevated position, it's gonna be. Can't stand sitting on it while that man waltzes into what used to be the Statehouse. Our statehouse. Wonder what they're gonna call it now."

"I'd think long and hard before taking action," Hutzman told him.

"She won't like it," Martine added. "Not one bit, and you tried every dirty trick you could think of when he ran against her. None of them worked."

"He's Teflon coated," Canton said. "Nothing sticks. Even the media down there is going easy on him. Public opinion's too strong in his favor. He's getting a free ride, and that ain't right" He heaved his bulk out of the chair and walked to the window, looking down over the White House lawns without seeing them.

"She wants him in there," Hutzman reiterated. "Don't know why, but she must have something in mind. She always does."

"Okay," Canton said, his back to them. "We can't take any shots at him, but she could help the other guy. What's his name? Green?"

"He doesn't stand a hope in hell."

"No, Billy," Martine said, "but David has a point. The president does nothing, and it looks like she doesn't care.

It's an open invitation to the other southern states. Secede any time you want, without any reprisals."

"Except a lack of financial assistance," Hutzman said.

"Doubt that they'd expect any. Barton obviously didn't."

"But that's what she wants, isn't it? To get rid of the Tea Party's base?"

"Yes, and she'll probably get it, but she's going about it the wrong way. The voters won't understand. They'll just think that Barton is walking all over her. If he can do that, why can't some Arab terrorist group or other?"

"Yeah, Edwina's got to do something," Canton insisted.

"Such as?"

"I don't know." Canton turned from the window and looked at Martine. "Hailey have any ideas?"

"Haven't discussed it with her."

"That's not a bad idea," Hutzman mused. "What you said just now, David. Something to do with Green, but she can't seem to help him get elected. That's ratifying the secession."

"She might as well do that," Canton said. "It's a done deal."

"Apparently so," the Speaker said. "But there must be some Georgians who didn't think it was a good idea. Maybe more than we know."

"People who'd like to return to the US?" Martine asked. "Yes, I'm sure there are, but Barton's not stopping them."

"Hard to leave your family and your friends, never mind your job or your business," Canton commented. "Some of 'em must feel like they've been given Hobson's choice."

"And what if Jerome Green is one of them?" Martine asked.

Canton and Hutzman stared at her.

"Is he?" Canton asked.

"Haven't the vaguest idea," Martine said. "Maybe he could become one if he stood to gain by it."

"Gain?"

"Yes, David. Gain by being the hero who reunited the union, and the governor of the state of Georgia."

"Think he'd go for it?"

"If she asked him, yes. She doesn't deal kindly with 'no'."

"But she won't."

"She might," Martine speculated. "What if we put it to her this way, he's not going to win, anyway, so what does it matter? She meets with him and discusses reunification, following his victory, and she's at least gonna get a lot of airtime and look as though she's in charge of the situation. What harm can it do?"

"None," said Billy Hutzman.

"Unless, of course, the dumb bastard wins," David Canton added. "She'd have us skinned alive if that happened."

Jerome Green held a press conference two days later. Striding up to the microphone was easy. Climbing onto the box that had been placed behind the podium, to maximize his height, and doing it without anyone noticing was a tad more difficult, but he'd practiced for over an hour the night before, and he thought he managed it rather well.

"Ladies and gentlemen of the press," he began.

"God," one of the reporters hissed to another, "every time he opens his mouth, I find myself thinking of Truman Capote."

The second reporter turned laughter into a snort, and Green stared at him for a moment, distracted by the sound.

"Ladies and gentleman," he repeated, 'thank you for coming here today. Yesterday, I travelled to Washington, DC, where I met with President Boulder. Video of that meeting will be made available to you all. What we discussed will, I think, have a momentous impact as our citizenry casts its votes next week."

The media perked up its collective ear, turned on recording devices and rustled through notebooks, looking for virgin pages.

"I had one question," Green said, "and one only. I asked the president what she would do if, following my election, I immediately requested that this so called Free State be readmitted to the Union in which it truly belongs."

Pandemonium erupted, and it was impossible for Green to distinguish any one question from the hundreds that were simultaneously flung at him. He held up both hands, begging for quiet.

"Please! Please! I'll be more than happy to answer your questions when my statement is finished, but not until then. Just let me get on with it."

The media reluctantly concurred.

"I am sure that many of our people will share my joy when I tell you that President Boulder magnanimously stated that she would be pleased if this should occur, and that no former Georgians would be in any way discriminated against. They would not, she said, be held at all responsible for the actions taken by one persuasive, grossly mistaken, and quite possible insane man. They will simply be American citizens once more, with all the privileges that entails.

"And what about you?" a TV reporter yelled.

"The president feels that the people will have spoken, and that it will be only right and proper that I serve as their governor. Please bear in mind that, while the majority of voters elected to secede, many voted against the proposition. Now, by voting for me, they will have a chance to correct this aberration and return to the great Union for which so many of their ancestors, not to mention their sons and daughters, have fought and died."

"All this happens if you win," another reporter pointed out. "What if you lose?"

"Should that happen," Green said, "and I do not think that it now will, I shall, with a heavy heart, leave the land of my birth and return to the country I love. I have been told, by the president, that anyone who joins me will be welcomed, and that I will be assured of a position in her government that will allow me to watch over, foster, and protect them. May God bless those who have the courage to walk with me, and may God bless America."

The reporters had so many questions that it was over an hour before Jerome Green left the podium. His legs were shaking by then, and he felt vaguely nauseous. What, he wondered, had he done?

"Wasn't prepared for this one," Jim Eliades said, staring at the TV in the kitchen at the Preserve, apparently unaware that he had turned it off once the Green segment of the news was over.

"When is Carolyn coming home," Catherine asked.

"Next week. Why?"

"You look as though you could do with a pair of loving arms around your shoulders right now."

Jim took a seat on one of the stools that lined the granite topped island, propped his head in his hands and ran his fingers through his hair.

"Don't like being blindsided," he said. "Feel like a fool. John's on his way. Just about had time for dinner at home. He was looking forward to that. Wonder if he's heard."

Dillon ran past them and down the passage to the back door, whimpering with joy as he went.

"Think we're about to find out," Catherine said.

John walked through the kitchen and out through the archway that led to the foyer, telling them that he'd be right back. He returned a couple of minutes later with three glasses and a bottle of bourbon. While Jim and Catherine watched, he poured drinks, added ice and water, and handed out the glasses.

"You two look as if you need this," he said. "Sip first, and then we'll talk."

The door in the conservatory opened, and Mike and Mellie came in.

"Don't need no talk," Mike said in the monotone his deafness had caused. "I'm gettin' pretty good at this lip readin' thing. Saw what you said right through that glass door. We all followed you to this new land, Mistah John, and we ain't going back 'less'n you tell us to. You gonna do that?"

"No," John said. "Can't somehow see myself doing that."

"I am not happy."

"No, Madam President, I am sure that you are not."

"If these figures are correct, and I am going to assume that they are, and if all the registered Democrats vote the party line, a negligible number of Republicans will have to join them in order for this man to win. It's unlikely to happen, but it is an unacceptable risk. I am not fond of unacceptable risks."

"I don't think that you have to worry, Ma'am."

"I wish I were as sure about that as you are, David. You told me that this man Green was an idiot, and that the press would place no credence in anything he said."

"I did, Ma'am, and the Speaker and your Chief of Staff agreed with me."

Billie and Martine shot him vicious looks, and Edwina's tone became even more threateningly even and cold.

"So you all discussed this? It might have been better if I had known that. Individually and jointly, you appear to have made a gross judgmental error."

"Madam President, maybe we could ... "

"Shut up, Billie. I find myself in a strange dilemma."

"And what's that, Ma'am?" Martine asked.

"I am relying on John Barton. No one else can save this situation."

John Barton requested live television time in the Free States that evening and, since there was still a distinct possibility that he might be its president, received it. The US networks did not hesitate to carry the broadcast.

John walked into the hotel ballroom and stood beside the podium. Without saying a word, he turned his back to the cameras, legs slightly spread, and bent over. He flipped the tails of his jacket up onto his back and remained in this strange position for a moment or two while the media gazed at him, open mouthed. He then straightened and went to the microphone.

"Tell me," he asked, "did any of you see a tail between my legs?"

Alone in the Oval Office, Edwina Boulder roared with laughter and applauded loudly.

chapter

TEN

It had to be the most publicized move in history. The media descended in droves on Greenville, South Carolina, packing hotels, restaurants, and bars, being lavish with their expense accounts and having a thoroughly good time. The city's business community would have erected a statue in honor of the Free State's new president, but they were afraid that D.C. might not like that.

By midday that Thursday, the sky was clear, the sun shone, and there was a pleasant hint of fall in the air. Convoys of vans and cars drove to the South Carolina side of the Lake Hartwell Bridge. The reporters and their crews crowded the grass verges, cradling their coffee cups and waiting while cameras were made ready and streaming links were established. The helicopters circling overhead reported on progress and, before long, the entire pack was staring southward.

The huge moving van was easy to spot. It was in the left hand lane, carefully observing the speed limit, and it obscured any vehicles driving behind it.

"Is he there?" a cameraman screamed into the headset that connected him to his network's bird. His stringer raised an interrogatory eyebrow, and was answered with a nod.

The van drove past, causing a rush of air and a lot of hair patting in its wake. The next vehicle was an American made SUV. In it were Jerome Green, his wife, their three children, and the family dog, who had his nose out of the window and was having a thoroughly good time.

"Free State presidential candidate, Jerome Green, has kept his promise," a reporter told the camera as the car sped by. "Following Tuesday's resounding defeat in his bid to govern the world's newest country, he has today, along with his family, come home to the U.S.A. We bid him welcome, but everyone here is surprised to see that none of his fellow Georgians have taken him up on his invitation and returned, with him, to the fold. We understand that Mr. Green delayed his departure by half an hour, anticipating that others would be traveling with him. He seems to have been mistaken."

"Poor man," Catherine Barton said. "I feel sorry for him, and more so for his wife and the children. He should never have made such a foolish public statement."

Her husband did not answer. He was on the phone.

Less than an hour later, John Barton was joined by Harris Gordon and Jim Eliades. They sat in the small office off the kitchen, with John behind his desk.

"Okay," he began, "we've had a day to recover. Now we need to get down to work. We have a country to run. Did you see the coverage of Green driving up eighty-five."

"Sure," Jim said. "Probably heading for D.C. Wonder what Edwina will do for him?"

"Not much of anything now that he's on his own," Harris said.

"I agree," John said, "but the coverage made me think of a few very important questions. I have a couple of others, on different subjects, and I'd like recommendations and guidelines as soon as possible. We should, I think, put together a couple of advisory boards, and we should do that very quickly."

"Fire away," Jim said.

"Beaufort Handler is going to remain governor, so he'll be in the Statehouse. Where will the Federal government be located? We can't continue to work out of The Preserve and the corporate offices. The nation needs a home for its president. Catherine and I are more than willing to stay here, but we're not moving out for the next occupant, so we need to work on that one, though it's not a high priority. We need office space in the Statehouse, and we need to decide whether to rename it, or leave it as it is."

"If other states join us, we'll have to rename it, or move to a more central location," Jim said, "but we can't decide that now."

"We still need to think about it," John told him, "and the rest needs to be considered right now. Those reporters were on the Georgia/South Carolina border. It used to be a line between two states. It is now a national border."

"Shit!" Harris Gordon said. "He's right. It is."

"So, do we allow crossings with only a driver's license, or do we require passports? We need crossing points on all the major roads. We need a border patrol. We need to design a Free State passport, and begin issuance immediately. Our citizens can no longer travel on their U.S. documents, and we don't want to impede either business or pleasure."

"We need to address Homeland Security," Jim said.

"And appoint a secretary to oversee it," John added. "We need to be prepared for embassy or consulate requests from other nations, and look into our representation on their shores. I don't think we can rely on the U.S. to come to the assistance of any of our citizens if there are international incidents, and we need to establish a customs and excise division. We have to take over our own airports, and the US officials need to go."

"They won't like that unless we can assure them that there is adequate security," Harris said. "They'll be worried about terrorists taking advantage of the new administration and entering the US via our country."

"Exactly," John said. "We need to get on this right away. Don't think either of you should plan on much sleep for the next few days, and neither should I."

"Just one thought, Mr. President," Jim said.

"Tell me."

"Maybe you should contact Dae-Jung Sun."

"Dae-Jung Sun? The Secretary General of the United Nations?"

"Yes. Even though we don't plan on joining, you might be able to get them to assist us with a speedy transition."

"Yes," John said. "I think I can do that."

Edwina Boulder fumbled for her cell phone, keeping her eyes tightly shut. She located it on her bedside table, attempted to grab it, knocked it to the floor, and swore as she sat up in bed, turned on the lamp, spotted the phone, and picked it up.

"This is the president," she mumbled. "What the hell time is it?"

"It's five-thirty, ma'am," Martine Rivers told her.

"Five-thirty? This had better be good."

"No crisis, ma'am. Just something I thought you should hear from me before you saw it on the news."

"Not even a choice between good news and bad news?" Edwina grumbled. "And I thought rank had privileges. Go ahead."

"The United Nations General Assembly has invited John Barton to speak at its next session, on Tuesday."

"Tuesday? What's wrong with Monday?"

There was a short pause before Martine said, "It's Veteran's Day, ma'am."

"Why the hell would they wanna do a thing like that?" Edwina demanded as she stalked into the Oval Office a mere twenty minutes later.

"I have no idea, Ma'am," Hailey Miles said. "The Secretary General's office released the announcement very early this morning, so President Barton must have accepted."

The president grunted a response, flopped into the chair behind her desk, and said, "Coffee."

Hailey poured her a mug and took it to her. Edwina cradled it and stared into its murky depths, lost in thought. Hailey perched on the arm of one of the sofas and watched her until she put the mug down, leaned back, stared at the ceiling, and said, "Something's going on. Get Martine, and David Canton, and Hutzman. Now. We need to talk. What time's my first appointment?

Hailey flipped through her iPad. "Nine."

"Good. Get on with it."

Edwina dealt with some of the ever present paperwork until she heard a discreet cough. She raised one finger, finished reading the sheet of paper she held, signed it, set it carefully to one side, and lifted her head. There was a quorum present.

Edwina set her elbows on the desk, clasped her hands, the fingers intertwined, and said, "I have not had a phone call from John Barton."

"But, Ma'am," Hailey said, "you didn't call him to congratulate him on his election."

"I would not congratulate that man if he were elected Pope," Edwina said. "May we continue without any further interruptions? I was not, contrary to what my press secretary seems to believe, expecting Mr. Barton to call to chat about the weather. I was expecting to be asked for money. Why has that not happened?"

"Maybe he went to the World Bank," David Canton said.

"Or the Swiss," Billy Hutzman added.

"Or perhaps some dot com tycoon has decided to classify him as a charity and donate billions," Edwina sneered. "If he had done either of those things, I'd know. I've taken care of that. No, something is going on, something I don't know about. That is intolerable. Find out what it is."

No one moved.

"Now!"

The United Nations General Assembly Hall is a massive room, three stories high, and capable of seating eighteen hundred people, none of whom feel crowded. The room is decorated in blue, and green, and gold; the colors of the sea, the sky, the land, and the sun; and it is filled, probably entirely intentionally, with a sense of sublime and pervading peace. Three tiers of balconies line the back walls, with seats for alternate delegates, guests, translators, and the media.

A dome crowns the room's high ceiling. Its interior is black, and it is filled with recessed lights. Even at midday, a visitor is given the impression that the stars themselves watch over the proceedings below. At the front of the room, on a raised podium, is the desk where the President of the General Assembly sits, with the Secretary-General of the United Nations to his right and the Under-Secretary-General for General Assembly Affairs and Conference Services to his left.

Behind them is a gold recessed panel, rising high, and displaying, in its center, the embossed UN seal, the globe as seen from the North Pole, flanked by olive branches, one of the universal symbols of peace.

Despite all this, the honorable delegates have been known to shout, indulge in name calling and, in one memorable incident involving Russian premier, Nikita Khrushchev, pound on the desk with a shoe.

Anything can happen at the United Nations, and it often does.

On a lower level of the podium, in front of the green marble desk, is a matching speaker's rostrum. It was there that John Barton stood, waiting for the welcoming applause to die down. He did not think it would take long. The Secretary General had just introduced him as the president of the world's newest nation, adding that he would speak to them about his country's foreign policy plans, and ending with, "Perhaps President Barton will also tell us why he has decided not to join us as we strive for world peace."

Silence fell rather remarkably quickly.

John looked around the room before he said, "Mr. Secretary General, honorable delegates, and guests, thank you for inviting me here today. I am, as the Secretary General has told you, the president of the world's newest country, a nation so young that some of you may fear I am not yet properly housetrained." A titter or two greeted this, and John ignored them and went on, "The opportunity to begin anew, to start from scratch, is not often granted to the citizens of any region of this earth. I know that my fellow Free Staters join me when I say that we give thanks to the Almighty for the gift we have been given, and that we are dedicated to creating the best country on earth in which to live, grow, meet a soul mate, raise a family, and enjoy peace and prosperity.

"We are fortunate. We have been able to watch the mistakes made by other nations, and learn from them. We have kept them in mind as we have worked to create our constitution and lay the groundwork for the laws that will insure domestic harmony. While we must, at this point in our existence, look inward with intense concern and concentration, we shall also look outward, for we are a part of the world community, and it is our duty to take our place in its hierarchy. We must formulate an international viewpoint, one that will guide our foreign policy.

"Let us then turn to the world as I, the first Leader of the Free States, see it today.

"Let me first address Russia, the largest remnant of what was once the USSR. Her government is corrupt, with few plans for the future. Her people are cursed with high alcohol addiction rates, a low birthrate, and an economy based on oil and gas exports. This economy can only decline. As we, and other nations, use fracking and angular drilling, and convert to more use of natural gas, we will reduce our need to import energy. Technological advances will increase self-dependence, and concomitantly decrease the need for Russian oil and gas both here and in Europe. Russia's economy will decline and, as the nation becomes poorer, it will become more unstable. We need to keep the Russian government in check, and pressure the USA and NATO to do the same.

"We are facing global water shortages, and China, in particular, will be seriously affected by them. I think it is very possible that the need for water will force China to begin the annexation of Russian Siberia. This will be, for the west, a distant war, and I do not foresee our military involvement. I am, however, concerned with the unintended consequences of this, or any other, war. Consequences with which the entire world will be forced to deal. China, at the same time as it fights this war, will be forced to face the results of another it has waged for fifty long years: The war against women. Half a century of penalizing the parents of female children, encouraging the demise of female newborns, and rewarding those couples who produce only one, male, child, will soon result in one hundred million young and virile men with no spouses. This, when coupled with a major conflict, will create a situation that can only be described as volatile."

John reached for a glass and took a sip of water, taking a rapid survey of the room as he drank. He was pleased to note that many of the delegates who had been lounging in their seats, half turned from him, were now facing him and listening intently to his words.

"I think I might be permitted to say that I have formed close personal friendships, over the last few weeks, with the leaders of India and Pakistan. Both these nations were among the first to recognize the Free States. India will continue to serve as a great balance to the power of China. She and Pakistan have recently been tempered in the flames of tragedy. It appears that they have overcome their religious differences and found a new unity. It is my hope and expectation that this new sense of brotherhood will enable them to work together to reconfigure the borders of Iran, Pakistan, and Afghanistan and create a region based more on tribal loyalty than the aims of an Islamic jihad. We may need to assist them as they encourage Iran's ethnic Azeri to join with the current Azerbaijani nation, producing a greater Azerbaijan. Similarly, the ten million Kurds now living in Iran, should link with Kurds from Turkey and Syria and form a new and powerful Kurdistan. I envisage this as a modern Islamic nation, like Azerbaijan, and one with which the west will enjoy cordial and peaceful relations.

"Once this is done, the world should turn its attention to Iran, and support the Persians remaining there as they replace a theocratic dictatorship with a modern Iran, free from the terrorists who are now in control, and the nuclear weapons they possess.

"From the Muslim nations, let us turn to the tiny state of Israel, another country that, very early on, extended the hand of friendship to my own. I thank them for that, and I recognize their importance as a homeland for Jews everywhere, and the custodians of so many sites that are holy for either Christians or Muslims. We can depend on Israel should it ever become necessary to take military action in the Middle East. We can depend on them to keep the international waterways open for transit, and we can rely on them coming to our defense should any other country decide to attack the Free States or the USA. It is imperative that we remain partnered with Israel in a shared defense agreement."

The members of the Israeli delegation were not the only ones who applauded this, and John conveyed his gratitude with a quick nod.

"I see the annexation of the Gaza Strip back into Egypt, behind whose borders it lay for thousands of years.

Much of the West Bank should then be incorporated into Jordan, and the remaining small area that is not part of Greater Israel should have its own borders created. It can then be designated as Palestine.

"I am now done with redrawing the map of the Middle East but, before I leave that region, I have one more statement to make, and it merits your full attention. The Free States will be a friend to modern Islam, but we will never tolerate Islamic radicalism. We shall never submit to Sharia law, not now, not ever."

There was more applause that died as several Arab delegations rose and left the room, taking their time and making sure that their action was noted. John watched them go, and did not say another word until the doors closed behind the final flowing robe.

"Now," he said, "let us turn to South and Central America. The Free States will join with like-minded nations there. Together, we will encourage and assist countries such as Venezuela, eventually welcoming them back to a free market economy, under the rule of just laws. If this cannot be accomplished, no one should be surprised if Columbia, whose territory it once was, retakes its old lands. For Cuba, the ever deteriorating proud jewel of the Caribbean, there is little hope until the Castro brothers are gone. Once this happens, we will encourage the new leadership to create a capitalist economy, invite foreign investment and help them to secure the energy sources they will have to import. A new spirit of hope will then surge through that oppressed island, it will begin national development, and we will welcome its government and its citizens as friends of the Free States.

"I had planned to address the current situations in Mexico, Europe and Africa, but I wish to leave time to answer the question the Secretary General asked when he was kind enough to introduce me to this august body. Why will the Free States not be joining the United Nations?

"On the face of it, there would appear to be no reason for us not to do this. This assembly has created what might be referred to as the world's largest level playing field. Each nation represented here, no matter how new, how small, or how poor, has one vote. Here, our voice would carry as much weight as that of the most powerful nation on earth. Here, we can be an equal partner in the formulation of international policy. Why, then, do we choose not to join?"

Many heads nodded in John's direction, as if the assembly as a whole were joining its Secretary General in asking the question.

"Because," John said, "there is no national resource we treasure more than our young men and women. They are the generation who will directly inherit this land we have created. They will be its guardians and caretakers, and they will foster its growth and prosperity. They will do this for their own children, and for all the generations to come. We shall, therefore, choose carefully any war in which we risk even one of their precious lives. We will not fight in conflicts deemed necessary by this body, but whose purpose we cannot fathom or comprehend. We look forward to a time when any war is truly being fought for the good of all humanity, and is worth the terrible sacrifices it demands. At that point, we shall proudly and with all due humility, request that these doors open to admit the wonder that is the Free States.

"Thank you, and may the Almighty bless each and every one of you and all that you strive to accomplish in this room."

John had expected to leave the podium quickly, his exit hastened by a mere spattering of applause.

The delegates instead rose to their feet and forced him to remain where he was for over two minutes. John smiled and waved, and turned to bow to the officials at the podium as they, too, stood to salute him.

"This is too much," Edwina Barton said. "Why don't we just name a new capital and proclaim this damned man World Premier?"

"Wouldn't say that in public," Billy Hutzman responded. "I'm afraid that too many people would think it was a good idea."

John's security detail was waiting for him directly outside the General Assembly Hall, and the men and women immediately formed a box around him, the living suit of armor that always made him vaguely uncomfortable. As they ushered him down the wide corridor, Jim Sparks, the head of the detail, took up a position to his right and spoke softly into his ear.

"We need to get you out of here ASAP, Mr. President."

"Was the speech that bad?"

The corners of Spark's mouth lifted an almost imperceptible degree, which was about as close as he ever came to a grin, and he muttered, "No, Sir, the speech was fine. You must have been able to tell that from the response, but you seem to have upset someone or other."

"Probably both," John said. "Tell me."

"We've had calls from Fox, CNN and most of the other news channels. Seems that some group, won't give a name, foreign accents though, has called each of them to say that you'll be dead by the end of the day. We need to get you home."

"Sounds good to me."

"Just let us guide you, Sir. We'll be leaving by a special route."

UN security guards lined the corridor, and one of them pressed a remote button as they approached. A section of the wall slid back, revealing a small and expertly concealed elevator.

"Not room for all of us to go with you, Mr. President," Sparks said. "Just you and me on this trip, but there'll be another detail waiting when the doors open."

John was about to step into the elevator when he heard his name being called and half turned to see a small Asian man running down the corridor, waving one arm in the air, and repeating, "President Barton, President Barton" as he hurtled toward them.

Before he knew it, John was flat on the floor, buried under heavy bodies, and the small man was in a similar position, his arms held behind his back, and his nose only inches from John's. John wondered if he looked as shocked and dismayed as the person in front of him, and was willing to bet that he did.

"Did you want to speak to me?" he asked, peering out past a navy blue suited arm.

"Yes, Sir. My name is Chung-Hee Woo, and I am the first assistant to the Secretary General. He wonders if you will do him the honor of joining him in his office for a meeting with him and his staff, and some light refreshment."

"I'd like to get up off the floor first," John said, "and I suspect that you share my ambitions. Excuse me. Sparks!"

"Sir?"

The voice came from somewhere above.

"Did you hear that?"

"Yes, Sir, I did."

"Do you have any reason to believe that the Secretary General of the United Nations plans to assassinate me?"

"No, Sir, I do not?"

"Then may this gentleman and I get up? I am sure that he is more than willing to show you his ID."

Sparks must have nodded, because the weight pinning John to the floor lifted, and hands were extended to help him to his feet. The same was done for Mr. Woo, who immediately indicated the name tag hanging from his lapel.

"My apologies, Mr. President," Sparks said. "Better safe than sorry. Shall we go?"

"Go?" John asked. "No, I don't think so. It would be churlish of me to refuse such a kind invitation."

"Then I must object, Sir. We cannot guarantee your safety here."

"Your objection is duly noted, Jim, and my thanks to all of you for your swift action. Now, Mr. Woo, are you recovered enough to show us the way?"

The office was high atop the tall building. Floor to ceiling windows turned one wall into an impressive panorama of New York's East River and the tip of Long Island jutting into the Atlantic Ocean. The other walls were paneled and, in places, lined with bookshelves. Dae-Jung Sun sat behind a contemporary, ten foot long desk, crafted of mahogany. His back to the view, he was gazing benignly over the top of steel rimmed glasses.

Appearances, John Barton thought as he took a seat in one of the Barcelona armchairs that faced the desk, really are often deceptive. Like his honored predecessors, Sun gave the impression that he was a man who preferred peace to war, a worthy man and, in all likelihood, a wise one. In fact, he had begun his political career as a protégé of Li Moon, the head of Korea's Grand National Party. Dae-Jung Sun took to political corruption as well as the proverbial duck takes to water. It was not to be wondered at. His father was a numbers runner, and Sun used the resultant connections with local law enforcement and judges, plus the fortune the old man had accumulated, to found a lobbying company that represented Korea's largest automobile, electronics, and insurance companies on an international governmental level.

Money, it is said, cannot buy love. Few of us would deny, however, that it can purchase a pretty reasonable facsimile thereof and, in much the same way, it can be used to create a cloak of respectability that covers and conceals many an ugly truth. No one knew this better than Dae-Jung Sun. He courted the media, throwing lavish parties at which talking heads were fawned over as if they were British royalty; he sent expensive gifts that were discreetly delivered, having passed through many channels between the giver and the recipient; and he was a vast font of phone numbers, some of them very private and others that connected successful men to young, lovely, and compliant Asian women. Mr. Sun liked to cover all the bases.

No-one and that is not an exaggeration, had ever read watched or heard a news piece concerning Dae-Jung Sun that had anything negative to say. Mr. Sun felt very positive about this.

If the man possessed a virtue, it was patience. He had not at all minded the almost three decades it had taken him to make the slow climb that ended at the door of this office. He had been young when he began the ascent, and he planned on enjoying the view for a nice long time. His terms of office each ran for five years, and John Barton was willing to bet that, although no man had ever served for more than a decade, Dae-Jung Sun was more than eager to set a precedent.

Sun nodded, as if he had somehow read John's mind and agreed with his conclusions, as he said, "Thank you for joining us, Mr. President. May I present my staff?"

John swiveled his chair around and listened as five names were listed, all of them, as far as he could tell, Korean. The four men and one woman who each bowed slightly as they were designated were seated on a long and comfortably upholstered sofa, note and ipads at the ready.

John nodded in acknowledgement and faced the desk again, saying nothing. The eyes that regarded him over the glasses were dark, impassive and quite remarkably reptilian. The thin lips curved into a well-practiced smile that conveyed a stunning illusion of sincerity, and the Secretary General quietly said, "So, President Barton, using war as an excuse, your mewling and quite insignificant, tiny country declines membership in the great world body we call the United Nations. May I ask why this is so?"

"Indeed you may, Mr. Secretary General, and I shall do my best to explain. As you so aptly remark, the Free States of America is small and insignificant. Nevertheless, we stand strongly behind certain principles and beliefs, many of which are not acknowledged within these esteemed walls. The world in general seems to me to take this body for granted, and to automatically accord it a veneration it perhaps does not merit. A closer look shows a dark vein running through the veneer of impartiality that covers the United Nations. It instituted a food for oil program with Sadam Hussein, while that evil man was torturing and murdering the citizens of Iraq. Bashar al-Assad, of Syria, was a member of the Commission of Human Rights while he was butchering thousands of those over whom he ruled. Libya and Iran were also represented on that Commission, even though Moammar Khadafy ordered and paid for the shooting down of a commercial airliner, causing the deaths of hundreds of its innocent passengers. Iran is a nation that tortures its citizens on a daily basis, executes women accused of adultery and murders homosexuals. We do not understand quite how all this equates with human rights.

"Neither do we comprehend your Palestinian policy. We want our citizens to be self-supporting, even if we must assist their first steps toward that goal. You have created on the Left Bank an entire population dependent on welfare, and the European nations who were supporting them are nearly bankrupt as a result. Without that money, what is to become of those you have made reliant upon it?

"But, Mr. President," Sun said, "do you have no compassion for the poor and hungry in sub-Saharan Africa, or for the starving children in Laos, Cambodia, and Burma?"

"We have the deepest compassion for each and every one of them, Mr. Sun, but that will not feed them or comfort them. We will not turn our backs. We shall do all we can for this world's troubled people, but I regret to inform you that we shall not do it through the United Nations."

Dae-Jung Sun rose from his chair and stood silhouetted against the light, his expression unreadable. "And you are very determined about this matter." It was not a question.

"Yes, Mr. Secretary General, I am. I foresee, and I shall encourage, the institution of a new global organization. It will be composed of countries that believe in national boundaries and sovereignty; that adhere to the rule of law, and that respect and encourage the freedom, peace and prosperity only a capitalist system can deliver."

"In that case," Sun said, "we should undoubtedly conclude this meeting."

There was a delay at Teterboro Airport, the New Jersey facility where John's jet had landed. Despite the security there, Sparks insisted that a very fine tooth comb be run over the plane from one end to the other.

Sparks and his crew breathed one sigh of relief when they landed in Atlanta, and another when they were behind the gates of The Preserve.

Catherine greeted John at the door. "This got here before you did," she said, kissing him and handing him a copy of a press release. "Doesn't sound quite accurate to me."

John glanced down at the paper. "So," he said, "Dae-Jung Sun and I have begun 'fruitful' talks aimed at the Free States eventually joining the UN and taking what he calls 'its rightful place among the world's nations'. Hope Jim doesn't have a dinner date with Caroline. This needs to be answered right away."

Catherine smiled and said, "Thought it might. Once that's done, I wonder if you could take a moment to explain these threats against your life."

"Oh, my darling," John said. "They are not the first, and I expect they will not be the last."

"That," Catherine Barton said, "does not make me feel any better whatsoever."

chapter

ELEVEN

The room was lit only by the flames crackling around the logs that lay in the wide fireplace. Heavy drapes were tightly drawn, and the only movement came from four fingers, tinted orange by the flames, that drummed quietly and in staccato sequence on the carved wood that trimmed a massive armchair.

One of the double doors silently opened, allowing light from the hallway to spill in, and the figure silhouetted against it crossed swiftly and silently to the chair. The fingers stilled and relaxed.

"Is it done?"

"Sadly, no. There was a tip off. Someone claiming to be behind the assassination attempt called the media."

"I see. That must be dealt with. No matter. We shall try again, and we shall keep trying until we succeed."

"Yes, I am sure that we shall."

"Tell Anderson that I shall be dining out, and make sure that I am entertained later in the evening. Asian, I think. Young, and virgin, and preferably frightened. I am not in a good mood."

Aside from a tendency to heavy jowls, a trait she deplored and blamed on her maternal grandmother who had, in her later years, somewhat resembled a disgruntled frog, Edwina Boulder had little in common with the nation's 37th president. She and the late Richard Nixon would have found it hard to establish ant mutual interest, unless they had jointly shared the Lincoln Sitting room. Nixon loved to work there, and Edwina regarded it as the only place in which she endeavored not to work at all. She liked to stretch out on the overstuffed sofa, a throw pillow behind her head, and let the warmth from the fireplace lull her into a doze.

Presidents, however, tend to be a tad short of dozing time, and Edwina had not visited her favorite part of the White House for a week or two, which was probably why she had decided that tonight's little encounter should take place there. That and the fact that, once the hall doorway was locked, the only entrance to the room was through the adjoining bedroom. Like naps, privacy was in short supply at 1600.

Edwina was curled in a corner of the sofa, wearing sweats almost the same color as its claret upholstery, when she heard the discreet tap on the door.

"Come. Did you lock the bedroom door?"

"Yes, Madam President."

Edwina patted the sofa cushion, and Martine Rivers sat down at the other end, ankles neatly crossed.

"It's just us. Be comfortable."

"Thank you, I will. It's been a long day."

Martine shook off her high heeled pumps and massaged each slim and elegant foot before she placed it on the sofa, bent her knees, wrapped her arms around her legs, and propped her chin at the apex of triangle thus formed.

"You wanted to see me?"

"Obviously. I need you to do something for me."

"Anything."

"You're quite sure about that?"

Martine met the eyes of the most powerful human being on the face of the earth and tried, without success, to get some inkling of what was to come next. There was a noticeable hesitation, and Edwina raised her eyebrows and waited.

"Yes."

"Good. Engela Metz is due here tomorrow."

"Yes, ma'am, the Chancellor's plane leaves Berlin in just a few hours. We reviewed the schedule with you this morning. Do you have changes?"

"Cut the 'ma'am' for the duration of this conversation. No changes. An addition."

"Addition? I'm not sure if that's possible. The Chancellor is on a tight schedule."

"She'll be staying in the Queen's Bedroom?" Edwina asked.

"Yes."

"And the State Dinner is the night before she leaves?"

"Right, and she has a private dinner with you tomorrow."

"Refresh me the other night?"

"She's free after cocktails at her embassy, and she has requested dinner in her room."

"Good. Make sure the wine is irresistible, give her half an hour, then take her some papers to review."

"What papers?"

Edwina looked exasperated. "I don't know. Does it matter? I'll think of something."

Martine lowered her legs to the floor and sat up straight. "So the papers are not the point of this exercise. May I ask what is?"

Their eyes met once again, and held until Martine released a small breath that might almost have been a sigh.

"I see. Is she ... .?

"I don't know, but we're going to find out. Wear that red dress with the slit that goes on forever. If that doesn't do it, nothing will."

Martine got up and walked over to the fireplace. She leaned a long arm the color of pale coffee on the mantel and gazed at the fire as she said, "Two questions, if I may. Is there a purpose to this, and do you find the thought of me prostituting myself for your convenience in the least disturbing?"

"Few whores earn even a tenth of your salary, and if you are asking if I shall be jealous, the answer is no. As to the purpose, it would be nice to have some measure of ... . well, shall we call it control, over the lady in question."

"You think that is necessary?"

Edwina considered before she said, "Yes, at this point I do. Which reminds me, see if you can find out where she's heading when she leaves here. They must file a flight plan at some point, though it'll probably be the last possible minute. She should go east, but I've a feeling she'll take a turn to the south once the plane's a few miles up and away from Andrews."

"South?" Martina looked puzzled for a split second, and then added, "Barton? Why?"

"Not sure ... but you can see that a little leverage might come in handy?"

"Yes, I suppose I can."

Edwina rose and crossed the room, unzipping the jacket of her sweats as she walked. "Normally," she said, "I'd leave this in your more than capable hands, but it has been a while, and I can't help feeling that a dress rehearsal, or perhaps an undressed one, might be in order."

Lukas Van Wycke's impeccably tailored tuxedo jacket enhanced his slim and attenuated frame, moving easily over his silk shirt as he reached out to accept yet another award. He hoped that he looked acceptably grateful and humbled, but he doubted that he could really manage either.

Van Wycke was one of the crown jewels of public broadcasting, and he had gleamed there for many decades. The son of the famous American heiress, Doris Page, and her first husband, a wealthy Dutch international business-man, Lukas spent the first few years of his life in Holland, moving to New York only after his parents were divorced. In the usual manner of the wealthy and privileged, he was educated at all the best schools, and he graduated magna cum laude from the proper vine covered university. After that, he spent a year seeing the world. Any oats he sowed there were not merely wild, they were tainted with ergot.

When Lukas Van Wycke returned to New York, it was obvious to Doris that her boy was gone. She found her-self facing, in his place, a tall man, with a sleek and aris-tocratic frame made for wearing good clothes. Pale hair swept over his forehead, highlighting piercing blue eyes and high cheekbones that curved from either side of a thin and somewhat long nose. Not surprisingly, given his bloodlines, Lukas Van Wyke was the quintessential WASP.

What was missing, Doris noted, was any trace of real humanity in those intelligent and observant eyes. It was rather frightening.

The next day, Doris and her son drove out of the city and up into the Hudson Valley. They visited relatives, at least figuratively speaking, dropping by the Roosevelt Presidential Museum, in Hyde Park, where Doris mar-veled once more over the sparsely furnished bedrooms and the rigorous childhood Franklin and Eleanor had imposed upon their offspring. A few miles up the road, they made a left and drove down a winding lane, canopied with trees. As they crossed a brook, the vast and ornate Vanderbilt man-sion loomed into view. Doris muttered, "So pretentious."

After that, they settled in for a long lunch at the Beek-man Arms, in Rhinebeck village. Reputedly the oldest hotel in the United States, the inn had welcomed guests since before the shot heard around the world was fired at Concord, Massachusetts. The building was well preserved and lovely, the food was more than good, and there were nooks convenient for private conversation.

Doris ordered a second martini when her son told her that he wanted a career in television, where he would indulge in political commentary.

A month later, Lukas Van Wycke's first show was broadcast. It was an instant hit, and its producers soon ceased blaming themselves for yielding to pressure from one of their most generous patrons. Doris could not believe how magnetic her son was. Leaning back in a large leather armchair, and looking down his nose at the camera, he ought to have been a repellent example of a spoiled brat. Instead, he was lucid and logical, interesting and illuminating, sage and surprising. The latter could probably be attributed to the fact that his politics were extremely left wing.

Lukas Van Wycke was, as conservatives often pointed out, a traitor to his class. "Ah," he was in the habit of sighing in response, "but then so was Cousin Franklin."

It was amusing at first, and many jokes were made about the anomaly of one of the country's richest men advocating the government's acquisition of money from those who had inherited it, married it, or just plain earned it, and the redistribution of the funds to those less fortunate. Lukas was more than willing to defend his views on shows hosted by pundits from the other side of the spectrum. When reminded that socialism had not worked in the USSR, in Cuba, in Venezuela, North Korea, Laos, Vietnam, or China, he peered down his nose, raised one corner of his mouth a fraction, and pronounced, "Did Einstein discard a theory because the first set of equations failed to provide proof? Did Edison abandon inventions when the prototype short circuited? Did Apollo 13's problems mark the end of space exploration? No, because they were simply experiments undertaken in the search for perfection. The same applies here, as I am sure you can well appreciate."

After that, few had the courage to point out that they did not.

By the time he was sixty, and Doris had long been languishing in the family vault, Lukas Van Wycke was a cornerstone of American life, and the accepted spokesman for the socialist progressive movement. He was also beginning to realize that he was running out of time. While conservative ethics allow a thick layer of cream to rise to the top of society, socialism equalizes the masses, thus permitting one, strong individual to reign over all. Lukas Van Wycke had been a drop in the cream since he drew his first breath. He wanted to stand alone.

Edwina Barton's husband's presidency had filled him with hope. Edwina's election made his fingers itch with the urge to grab what was so tantalizingly and nearly his. John Barton's had just the opposite effect. Lukas Van Wycke hated the very thought of the Free States of America.

Barton made far too much sense. If his system worked, and Lukas had a nasty suspicion that it would, each of his people would have an equal opportunity to rise as far as they were able, and enjoy the fruits of their labor unencumbered by excessive government or crippling taxation. When that happened, other states would leave the union, and those that remained would vote for candidates who offered plans similar to Barton's. After that, there would be no hope for Lukas Van Wyke.

He pulled himself back to the present, though it took some effort, concluded his speech of thanks, raised the new award high in the air, acknowledged the applause and left the stage. When he reached his seat, he was surprised to see a middle-aged woman seated to his right, where his PA should have been.

The woman leaned close to him once he was seated and said, in an undertone, "I'm Valerie Laughton. Please don't be angry with Peter. I needed a word with you, and I persuaded him to switch seats. He's young, and he still finds it hard to say no to his favorite aunt."

Lukas Van Wyke said nothing.

"You see," the woman went on, her breath unpleasantly moist in his ear, "I am the head of Freedom From Fear, you must have heard of us. Freedom from want, freedom from oppression, freedom from war, and a few others we add from time to time. I'm hosting a symposium on world poverty, in Sun Valley, next July. There's an emphasis on medical care for the economically disadvantaged, and we would be thrilled if you would consent to be one of our key-note speakers."

Van Wyke stared at the person at the microphone as if he were a young and nubile blonde, rather than an over-weight and boring CEO.

"We've tried to include a variety of viewpoints," the woman continued, not at all daunted. "We've even invited that fascinating John Barton. Have you met him?"

Lukas Van Wyke waited until a smattering of applause died away before he said, "No, I have not had the pleasure. He will be there?"

"Yes, he accepted almost at once."

"Interesting. Much as we differ, I think it time that President Barton and I meet face to face. Yes, I find I shall be honored to attend. Kindly provide Peter with the exact dates and the schedule."

There was an audible gasp of surprise before the woman suggested, "Perhaps you should check first. I'd hate to find that you had a conflict?"

"I assure you, Madam, that there is no possibility of such an event. You have become an absolute priority."

Lukas Van Wyke was horrified when he realized that he had been redundant.

"Jamaica! What the hell is she doing in Jamaica?"

"According to the German press, Ma'am, she has rented a house in Ochos Rios for a couple of days. There's even a picture of her sunbathing on the beach."

"Maybe I'll join her," Edwina Boulder grumbled. "I could use some R 'n R."

"Would you like me to make the arrangements, Madam President?"

"Oh, ferchrisake, Martine, you know I can't do that. What happened last night?"

'Nothing."

"Well isn't that terrific. How come?"

"I did exactly as you asked, down to the red dress."

"And?"

"And the Chancellor complimented me on it, and said she had noticed it at the cocktail party at the embassy. She asked me for the designer's name and made a note of it."

"I'm sure this is fascinating," David Canton said, waddling over to the desk and picking up the magazine Martine had placed there, "but I'm not into haute couture. Mind if I borrow this until we get back to politics?"

Edwina waved him away, and he shrugged and took a seat on one of the Oval Office's two long sofas.

"Go on," Edwina commanded.

"Well, she rubbed her neck, and I asked if she'd like a massage. Told her I did the same for you. She politely declined, and I could tell she was waiting for me to leave."

"Did you?"

"No. I asked if she had enjoyed the wine, and told her I was responsible for the selection. I said I'd heard it was wonderful, but I'd never actually tasted it."

"So she had to offer you a glass."

"Yes."

"This is getting better," the president said. "Go on. I can hardly wait."

"This was worth the wait," Engela Metz said, glancing around the study at The Preserve. "Such a lovely room."

"Thank you, Engela. Come, sit by the fire. Catherine and Mellie will bring tea in half an hour or so. We can talk until then."

"We shall probably talk for most of the night, John Barton, for I must leave very early tomorrow."

John sat down opposite the tiny German Chancellor, who appeared to be in danger of sinking into the soft chair and disappearing from view. He smiled and said, "The first time I met you, Engela, you amazed me. I regret to say that our second meeting has begun with a disappointment."

Engela Metz leaned forward, frowning in puzzlement. "How so, John? Disappointment? How so?"

"Well, I had thought that I would welcome my first visiting head of state at the airport. Band, honor guard, red carpet, flowers, cameras, and a cheering crowd. I was rather looking forward to it."

Engela laughed. "And, instead, she sneaks up to your back door, wearing a black wig, and has to remain hidden in your house. My poor John. Do not worry. The next time you shall have all your, what do you call it, shells and whistles?"

"It's usually bells, but I think I might prefer shells from now on."

"Shells," Engela said. "Cowry shells. Did you know that they were once used as money in many regions of the world?"

"I think I've read about that," John said. "And I can only admire such a subtle segue into the reason for your visit."

"I," Engela Metz said, "am about as subtle as an ICBM."

"You'd like people to think that, Madam Chancellor, but it is far from the truth."

Engela Metz smiled at the president of the Free States of America. "You are a wise man, John Barton," she said. "Come, let us talk business."

"Then she shook my hand," Martine said, concluding her report of her encounter with Germany's Chancellor. "She told me that she had enjoyed meeting me, thanked me again, and said goodnight."

"Damn," Edwina Boulder said.

"Damn."

"I don't need a parrot, David."

"Who does? Noisy, dirty things."

"What are you talking about?" Martine asked.

"Parrots. She brought them up."

"She?" Edwina asked, drawing out the vowel.

"Sorry, Madame President, but you need to look at this."

"What?"

David Canton pried himself up from the sofa and hauled his bulk to the desk. He set the magazine he had been reading in front of Edwina and pointed to a photograph of a woman reclining on a chaise, a large hat and dark glasses shading her face, and her bikini clad body, glistening with oil, basking in the sun.

"That's not Engela Metz," he said.

"According to the caption it is," Martine protested. "And it looks like her."

"Can't see much of the face, though," Edwina said.

"Don't need to," Canton told her. "Look at the belly."

"The belly? Why?" the president asked.

"Spent some years as an ambulance chaser," Canton told her. "Right out of law school. You pick up bits and pieces of medical knowledge when you handle cases like that. Just bits and pieces, but they add up."

"To the Chancellor of Germany's abdomen?" Edwina asked.

"No, to someone else's."

"David, you have two seconds to be specific. After that, you can leave this office."

"Okay, Ma'am. Engela Metz, if I recall rightly, has two children. This woman has never carried a child."

"Oh, God," Martine gasped. "He's right. There's no line down her belly."

"And no stretch marks," Edwina added.

"So," Canton said, "where in hell is Germany's own steel magnolia?"

Edwina Boulder picked up the phone.

Catherine Barton tapped on the study door, opened it and inserted her head and shoulders into the room.

"John, Madam Chancellor, please excuse me for interrupting, but Edwina Boulder is on the phone."

"Gott in Himmel!" Engela gasped. "Does she know that I am here?"

"I think so," Catherine told her. "She asked to speak to either or both of you."

"Could be a bluff," John said. "I'll take it."

He went to the antique French desk and picked up the phone. "Madam President, this is John Barton. How are you today?"

"I am puzzled, Mr. President, and I don't like being puzzled."

"So you have called me for assistance? I'm flattered."

"Don't be, Mr. Barton. I wouldn't have bothered if I had not been sure you had the answer."

"Hard for me to know that, Edwina, until you ask the question."

"Why is an unknown woman lying on a beach in the Caribbean pretending to be Engela Metz?"

"And you somehow feel that I can answer that?"

"If you can't, why don't you ask the Chancellor?"

"Ask the Chancellor?" John repeated, doing a good job of sounding perplexed.

Engela Metz walked over to the desk and tapped the speaker button.

"Would you mind repeating the question, Madam President?"

"Not at all, Madam Chancellor," Edwina said, and she did.

"The answer is simple," Engela told her. "She is there because I pay her to be there. The person in question is a distant cousin, who happens to rather closely resemble me. She has, shall we say, replaced me on several occasions when I have felt the need for privacy."

"And you felt this need today."

"Yes."

There was silence, and Engela smiled at John.

After a moment, Edwina said, "The currency. Your new currency, Barton's going to use it."

"Yes, Madam President. I am."

John held out his right hand, and Engela shook it.

"Thank you," she said. "You, Madam President, have shortened our meeting, and ended our discussions. President Barton has just given me his hand. Knowing that he is a man of honor, I consider this to be a concrete agreement. Now, instead of talking all night, I can enjoy a leisurely dinner with John and Catherine, and a good night's sleep. Thank you."

"I would think again," Edwina said, "were I either of you. This will not make me happy."

"We apologize for that," John said, "but each of us must think of the good of our own people first."

"Offending the most powerful nation on earth is seldom good for any people," Edwina said. "Offending that nation's leader is foolish. I consider your actions to be dishonest, filled with duplicity, and invasive."

She hung up the phone.

"Invasive," Engela echoed. "Explain to me, John. Is this not an odd choice of words? Did she mean evasive."

"No," John Barton said. "I don't think she did."

Lukas Van Wyke strolled along the banks of the river, enjoying the beauty that surrounded him even though the English air was damp and chilly.

"The Thames is lovely at this time of the year," he remarked to the young man walking beside him.

"It somehow manages to be lovely whatever the season, and this stretch, or reach, of it, sir, is properly called the Isis."

"Really", Van Wyke said. "I didn't know that."

They approached a bench, and Van Wyke seated himself and looked up at the young man. He was tall, with his mother's dark eyes and hair, slim, good looking, aristocratic, and obviously privileged. Van Wyke had seen to that.

"How are your studies progressing," he asked.

"Well, I think, sir. Post-graduate work at Nuffield is far from easy, but I don't mind economics, and political science fascinates me, so I seem to do well."

"So a doctorate by the end of this year?"

"Yes, if all goes as planned." The young man grinned. "You must be looking forward to it, sir, all these years of paying for my education coming to an end. You have been so generous, and so kind. I don't know how I can ever repay you."

"It has been a great pleasure," Van Wyke said. "As to your last statement, if you would sit down for a moment, I think I can tell you."

The young man took a seat at the other end of the bench, and Van Wyke shifted so that they were facing one another. A scull passed them, moving silently through the water. They could hear the rower's labored breath and see it steaming in front of him. Traffic hummed in the distance, and the spires of Oxford pierced the sky behind and before them. A bird trilled, and the sun blazed for a moment before it hid behind yet another cloud.

"Martin," Van Wyke began, "do you have any memories of your parents?"

"No, sir, none. I was only six when the accident happened."

"Yes, six. Can you remember other things from that time?"

"Yes," Martin Wickham said. "Clearly. I remember the house, and the garden with the high wall around it, it's not far from here, is it? And I remember Paula who came to take care of me."

"When did she arrive?"

"Right after the accident, I suppose. And you. You were always there."

"So, Martin," Van Wyke said. "You recall events after the accident, but nothing before it. Does that not strike you as odd?"

"I've never really thought about it. I wasn't in the car, was I, so that can't be trauma caused? It is odd, now that you come to mention it. Sometimes I think I can remember my mother, but that may be just from looking at photos."

"It isn't." Van Wyke took a deep breath and added. "Martin, I am your father."

"You? But what about the accident?"

"There was no accident, Martin."

The young man stood up and stared out over the water. When he turned back, the color had left his cheeks and his eyes were bright and hard. "I think, sir," he said, "that you have some explaining to do."

It was over an hour before the two men retraced their steps. The sun was beginning to sink, and Van Wyke was very cold.

"So there you have it," he said. "All of this was done to protect you, so that you could grow without the notoriety of belonging to one of the richest families in America, without being labeled the bastard child of a scandalous relationship with another man's wife, without the pressure of having my mother as your grandmother."

"Is Amelie still alive?"

"No."

"And the Comte de Grenois?"

"He also is dead. He took her back after you were born. They were a Catholic family. No possibility of a divorce, and he needed both an heir and the very generous settlement I provided."

"So she sold me."

"No, she did what honor demanded she do. I think it broke her heart, and later her spirit. You were only a few weeks old when she left."

Van Wyke walked a few paces, allowing Martin to digest this before he went on, "So I bought the house here, and Sheila arrived. She was the woman in the photos, the woman you thought of as your mother. She took such great care of you, and she loved you. In the end, she loved you too much. She began to think of you as her own, to fight with me over raising you and your future, so she had to go. I invented the accident, and Paula came."

"I still don't understand why you never told me," Martin said. "Or why you are telling me now."

"Because, my son, it is time for you take your place beside me. Your place in the world."

Saint Mark's was filled with white lilacs, calla lilies, peace roses, and Queen Anne's lace, all out of season or only grown in other climes, and all flown in because the bride loved them.

Organ music played, and the guests had all arrived, filling the pews. When the music stopped, Jim Eliades took his place at the altar and the vestibule doors opened to reveal Carolyn, on John Barton's arm. The guests rose to their feet, the first notes of the Trumpet Voluntary filled the air, and the slow walk down the aisle began.

Carolyn was radiant. Her gown was fashioned of white lace as fine as a spider's web. The tiny jewels sewn into it sparkled as the lace moved, making it seem as if the woman wearing it was floating. The veil that flowed from Carolyn's pearl encrusted hair streamed into a train behind her and was held by three small boys and three girls, each of whom had needed A Mother's Love, and each of whom had found it.

When they reached the altar, the children set the train on the carpet as if it were as precious as their Carolyn, and solemnly, hand in hand, walked to their assigned places. John Barton lifted the veil that covered the bride's face, carefully placed it behind her, kissed her cheek, and walked over to Jim. The guests who had wondered at the lack of a best man wondered no longer.

For Jim and Carolyn, the ceremony took place in a world only they occupied, and in which there was little except each other's eyes. They returned to reality only when the Wedding March played and they walked up the aisle.

The reception was held at The Preserve. Champagne flowed, buffet tables were laden with succulent dishes, piles of gleaming fruit, shrimp and lobsters, and yet more flowers. A band played, couples danced, children played and giggled, and Jim and Carolyn exuded happiness. It settled on the guests as if it were fairy dust, and no one would ever forget that day.

When it was over, John and Catherine sat, with their children and their families, in the study, enjoying a nightcap and the chance to be together. The little ones fell asleep in chairs, on sofas, or in their parents' arms, and the adults spoke softly, loath to wake them.

"I swear the kids painted themselves with that wedding cake," Miranda, the Barton's oldest son's wife, said. "They are raspberry stained from head to toe."

"Don't blame them," her husband, Jack, told her. "That filling was delicious."

"All the food was fabulous," Ellie Barton Payne said. "Where did you find those caterers, Mom?"

"Caterers?" John Barton exclaimed. "You should know better than that, Ellie. Mellie and your mother worked for days on that food. I don't think there *is* a caterer who can cook like they can. The only help they'd let me hire was servers and the clean-up crew."

"Mom," Foster said, "the older I get, the more I realize how truly amazing you are."

"Not me, darlin'," Catherine said, smiling at him. "You want an amazing woman, you start with Carolyn McKay."

"Carolyn Eliades now," Miranda put in.

"Yes," John said, "and she's the best thing that could have happened to Jim."

"Think that goes both ways," Ellie's husband, Christopher, said.

"Always good when it does," his wife told him. You know, the more I get to know Carolyn, the more I admire her. Imagine taking your honeymoon with ten children in tow. Only Carolyn would do that."

"And manage to make Jim think it was a great idea," Foster added. "There'd have been no chance of that a year or two ago."

"He loves her so much that ... " Catherine had no chance to finish the sentence. The door to the study burst open.

"Thought so," Dallas Dee Trelawny said. "Family gatherin'. There's some of us still here that kinda thinks we're family, too. Sure would like your company. Get your butts up, and leave those kids. Mellie 'n' I'll tuck 'em in upstairs. You moms and dads can either spend the darned night or pick 'em up in the mornin'. S'up to you."

"Yes, ma'am," John said, rising to his feet. "I may be the president, but I've more sense than to argue with a determined woman, let alone a Texan one."

"Cut the crap and follow the noise," Dallas told him.

They did, and they found the kitchen full of Saint Mark's board members, its pastor, Mellie, Tom, and their children, and Harris and Tilly Gordon. People were picking at leftovers, talking, laughing and sipping drinks.

"There they are," Harris roared. "Someone pour our president a bourbon. Bet he's had enough of that bubbly swill."

"Make him a Cuba Libra," Ramon Hernandez said. "A real drink for a real president."

Someone found the Bose radio and turned it on. Within minutes, couples were dancing in the crowded space.

"Seems like we're having a party," Catherine Barton said as Jack, her oldest son, pulled her into his arms and the rhythm of a waltz. John bowed to Miranda extending his hand, and she was only too happy to accept the unspoken invitation.

Mellie tapped Tom on the shoulder and, when he turned to face her, said, "Gonna make some coffee. Seems like some of these folk will need it pretty soon."

Tom, who had become a good lip reader, nodded. He felt a hand on his shoulder and turned to find Foster standing there.

"Good to see you, Tom," he said. "Feeling good?"

"Sure am, young Foster," Tom said. "You done muscled up on me."

"Sailing will do that for you, Tom, and I needed it. God, I was a skinny little runt."

"That you were," Tom agreed. "Good to see the family together again, ain't it?"

"Yes, Tom, it is. Though it doesn't seem quite right without Jim and Carolyn."

"Heck, Foster, can't ask them to interrupt their honeymoon to fool around with us."

Foster laughed and said, "Guess we could ask, but doubt it would do us much good. Mom's kitchen doesn't stand much of a chance when compared to a beach house on a tropical isle."

He looked around the room, then froze, his hand tightening its grip on Tom's shoulder. Tom followed his gaze and gasped.

Jim Eliades stood in the open double doors that led to the foyer. No one else had yet noticed him, but they began to, one by one, and the room grew quiet.

"Jim," Catherine said. "What are you doing here? Where's Carolyn? Is she all right?"

"She's fine," Jim said. "She's with the children."

He went to John and laid a hand on his arm. "Mr. President," he said. "It is my sad duty to inform you that United States' troops are massing on all our borders."

"What?" John asked. "When did this happen?"

"We were on our way to the airport," Jim said. "One of the kids was playing with Carolyn's iPhone. He was on Facebook. There are posts from people who can see the troops. They're scared. You might want to come to the Capitol."

"No time," John said. "We'll deal with it here."

He kissed Catherine, squeezed her hand, and headed for the study. Jim and Harris followed him. Catherine's children clustered around her. Tilly Harris placed an arm around her shoulders, and Mellie took one of her hands.

Catherine Barton reached out to caress hair, stroke cheeks, and pat arms.

"Look at you now," she said, serene and smiling. "You look as if you have something to fear. You don't. Your father is here, our president is here, and he will prevail. He can do nothing less, for God is walking beside him."

"Amen," Mellie said, and the others echoed her, filling the air with prayer.